T0332531

A
GREEK
LOVE

Also by Zoé Valdés

Yocandra in the Paradise of Nada
I Gave You All I Had
Dear First Love
The Weeping Woman

A GREEK LOVE

A Novel of Cuba

ZOÉ VALDÉS

*Translated from the Spanish
and with a translator's note by*
DAVID FRYE

Arcade Publishing • New York

For Giorgos

For Attys Luna, Tonino, and Gilberto *(Bel Ami)*,
remembering Crete

That is for the future. We only take care of now.
Tomorrow is out of our hands.
Sophocles

In the clamor in which we live, love is impossible
and justice is not enough.
Albert Camus

Translator's Note

This short, lyrical novel opens with a walk that the protagonist, Zé, takes through La Habana Vieja, the original
core of Cuba's capital and largest city, from the Malecón
seawall to her family's tiny one-bedroom apartment in one
of the moldering nineteenth-century mansions that had
been converted, generations before the revolution, into
tenement housing for the poor and working class of the
city. You can follow the exact route that Zé takes through
the city—if, that is, you know which Old Havana land-
marks have moved since the 1970s, like the Regla ferry
dock; which have changed names, like the Parque Habana
(renamed Plaza Vieja in the 1990s); and which have disappeared altogether, like the Cine Habana. By re-creating
these details, and doing so with a language filled with
Cuban and Havana slang—in the Spanish, that is; there is
no real way to duplicate the effect in any other language—
Zoé Valdés stakes a claim to literary ownership of the
island whose government pushed her into exile nearly
three decades ago.

A Greek Love opens in the Havana of Cuba's "gray

years" (*el quinquenio gris*), the mid-1970s, when the authorities responded to the crushing failure of their economic plans by imposing a strict, almost Stalinist regime of cultural repression and sexual conformity on the country. As Zé's story shows, all was not well behind the scenes. When she tells her parents that, at age sixteen, she had gotten pregnant by an equally young son of a Greek ship's captain, her father bursts with a rage that he has to keep carefully muffled, in a pretense of not letting the neighbors find out. The scene reveals her father's domestic violence and sexual hypocrisy, and also shows her father's (and Cuban society's) inward-turning distrust in the 1970s of the foreignness symbolized by Greek sailors in the nearby port of Havana. Fear of informers, tempered by the dangling carrot of advancement within the system, is enough to keep people in line, though. Publicly, at least, silence reigns.

The next scene shifts thirty-three years ahead, to the go-go years of 2008 or 2009, when, as Zé observes inwardly, "the gangsters who stole democracy on the island had decided to stop being rabid communists and had turned instead into savage capitalists." The scene takes place in a sterile, hermetically sealed, air-conditioned office—the physical opposite of the decaying tenement scenes in the first chapter—where Zé is being interviewed by a government functionary. Emblematic of the times, it is impossible to tell throughout the interview whether the bureaucrat is acting in his old function as an agent of the state police or in his new guise as an aspiring entrepreneur; as he speaks, he flits back and forth effortlessly between the two personas.

Subsequent chapters alternate between the storyline from the past and the novelistic present of the early 2000s. In the first time line, the young and pregnant Zé moves from the capital to the provincial city of Matanzas—less than sixty miles from Havana, though it takes her an agonizing twelve hours to get there on board the ancient electric train built in the early 1900s by the Hershey corporation to bring sugar from their plantations to the ports. In Matanzas, under the watchful and maternal eyes of her aunt, mother, and mother's lover, she gives birth to a son, Petros, who goes on to become a musical prodigy. Growing up in Matanzas, Petros specializes in the rural music of the region, which he plays on the *tres*, the three-chord guitar typical of those genres. But with the help of his three mother figures, he also picks up the small, lute-like Greek bouzouki, combining the folk musical forms of his twin heritages in an implicit rebuke to the cultural isolationism and xenophobia that had marked his earliest years. The second time line follows Zé as she prepares for, and in part two of the novel goes on, a much-anticipated first trip off the island. Traveling to the Greece that she had for so long dreamed of seeing, she meets for the first time in decades the Greek lover who gave her a son.

The novel creates a counterpoint between two types of "Greek love": *agape*, the selfless loving-kindness that Zé and the women in her life shower on Petros and which he returns in kind; and *pathos*, the passion she felt for her young Greek lover, which she never quite recaptures—though she comes tantalizingly close in her relationship with an older Greek man in the second part of the book. In some ways, *A Greek Love* is a counterpoint to Zoé Valdés's quasi-autobiographical second novel, *Yocandra in the Paradise of Nada*, which she wrote early into her exile in Paris in 1995. The protagonist of the earlier novel, the Yocandra of the title, whose life trajectory mirrors Zoé Valdés's own, even makes a cameo appearance in *A Greek Love* as Zé's childhood friend, schoolmate, and long-distance correspondent. But Zé is not Zoé, despite the similarity in their names; or if she is, she's the Zoé who never left Cuba, the alter ego that almost every Cuban in exile seems to wonder about: who would I have been, if I had stayed?

A
GREEK
LOVE

PART I

Petros,
or
ἀγάπη

TWILIGHT SPREAD ITS colors across the Havana bay. Zé sat on the seawall sunk in thought and contemplated the purple-tinged sky. The sea glimmered golden, rimmed with a coppery, tarry foam. She tucked her legs in front of her and wrapped her arms around them where she sat, just steps from the Regla ferry dock. The descending sun dissolved like butter into the waves on the horizon. At the same time the thick foaming swell of the blue sea seemed to give birth to the moon's transparent oval, rising at the same mellow, ghostly pace at which the sun opposite it was falling. The two gleaming, blinding lights crossed precisely at the center of a sky as resplendent as a painting, placid and exact, at the very moment she was telling herself she'd never seen such a sky as this, had never imagined a heavenly dome like this could exist anywhere in the universe, painted in the most unanticipated hues, from the purest, most innocent blue to the guiltiest, most brutal scarlet.

Night caught her in the same pose: arms wrapped round her legs, staring into the horizon. Surrounded now by darkness, she heard the musicality of the waves, as if they were performing just for her, while from the east she heard the roar of the ocean proclaiming a distant storm. Overhead, though, for a short while the sky was still clear, enormous, full of stars. It was only when she noticed the distant flashes of lightning that she decided to go back home.

She crossed the boulevard, turning in the direction of the convent of San Francisco de Paula, and paused in front of the Fuente de los Leones. The carved lions had always looked rather feminine to her. Why, instead of lions, had it not occurred to them to carve dolphins from alabaster? She smiled and pronounced the word softly, syllable by syllable: "A-la-bas-ter."

"What's the Parthenon like?" she had asked Orestes not long after they met.

"Marble and alabaster," he answered simply.

That word "alabaster" sounded to Zé like the most beautiful in the world. Orestes's frugality with words didn't surprise her—he spoke Spanish but sometimes he became tongue-tied, so he preferred to leave things unsaid rather than make grammatical errors; besides, he wasn't highly educated as she had imagined most Greeks would be.

She walked along Mosquito Park, across from the old Customs House building, then turned into the darkness of Calle Muralla, the street she lived on. She passed the house where Alexander von Humboldt had lived much more than a hundred years before. A few blocks later she turned into number 160, leaving the Parque Habana and the Cine Habana behind.

The tenement was unlit, as always. The bare bulbs that dangled in the hallways and the lamps in the common areas had been smashed by neighborhood gangs of rock-throwing kids. The damp staircase stank of pooled excrement and urine. Piss and feces of the second-story neighbors, fifteen families, more than a hundred people all told, oozed from the ceiling. The bathroom drain had been clogged for over a decade; no one who lived there could afford the repairs, and the government never offered any help. She sidestepped the drain spouts that tainted everything they touched with earthy, foul-smelling stains.

Finally, she reached the room where her father sat waiting for her, rocking his wide wooden armchair, *swish-swoosh*, *swish-swoosh*, *swish-swoosh*, in the shadows, his thick leather "bully-tamer" belt slung across his knees.

Her mother lay on the old bed pretending to be asleep, acting like it didn't matter that her daughter had come home so late, hoping that her husband, Gerardo, would come with her to bed instead of turning violent, the way he usually did. Her younger brothers lay on rickety but clean cots, snoring.

"Where the hell you been?" he demanded, angry but restraining himself, brandishing the belt menacingly.

Her mother leaped up and stood between them. "Leave her alone, Gerardo, she's almost a full-grown woman. Don't whip her!"

"Shut your trap, Isabel. That girl's driving me up the wall. Dragging herself in here like a whore so the whole neighborhood'll be talking about us, pointing their fingers at us. They'll fire me at work! She's gonna fuck up my Party membership! Don't you see? Can't you see? She's just trying to get on my nerves! She's gonna ruin my life, that . . . that . . . that son-of-a-bitch daughter of yours!"

"She's your daughter, too, bastard!"

Up to that point Isabel had been gently patting the arm that held the frayed belt, trying to calm him down, but her attitude changed when she heard the insult, though she kept doing all she could to restrain him.

He brusquely shoved her aside. Deaf to his wife's pleas, he gave her a flick of the belt, then laid into their daughter. The leather smacked the arm that Zé had raised to protect her face from the buckle; she already had too many scars on her legs and refused to give him the luxury or the pleasure of cutting her cheeks, too. Yet she didn't let out so much as a whimper or let her face show pain. Instead, she puffed out her chest, squared her shoulders, showed courage, made herself taller, upright, proud, and angry as she faced up to him.

"Mamá, Papá, I have to talk to you. It's serious. I need you to really listen to what I've got to tell you. I know you won't like it. Especially you, Papá, you won't like it at all," she said in clipped phrases.

Her father took a few steps back and fell into the rocking chair, exhausted. He whined almost comically about a pain he felt on the left of his chest, lifting his hand to squeeze his breast through the wide white undershirt that he wore.

Zé panicked at the thought she might have given her

father a heart attack. But no, that wasn't it, just more of the old man's theatrics.

"Stop piling it on, don't be so dramatic!" her mother agreed.

The little ones woke up and jumped from their cots, rubbing their eyes, accustomed to the annoyance of scenes like this between their father and big sister.

Embarrassed in front of the kids, Zé tried to shield them from witnessing yet another quarrel between her and their father, but how could she? She had to confess her dark secret right away, and there was no choice for her but to do it in front of the boys. She had no place else to go and talk to him where the young ones wouldn't hear. The room they lived in was too narrow. Where else to go? Where could she hide them? In the end, she decided to speak.

"Papá, Mamá, I'm . . ." She glanced furtively at the kids, who stared in fear, perhaps because they guessed she had something more terrible than usual to say. Pavel, the youngest, held his forearm over his eyes to keep from witnessing the storm. She plowed ahead. "I'm, well, you haven't noticed, but, I mean—what I'm trying to say is, I'm pregnant."

"What did she say, Isabel? What did that girl say? What did you say, you little shit?" Gerardo's face suddenly regained its composure, a weird, disturbing calm, as he turned pale and his teeth began to chatter.

The young woman could see that he was keeping his fury in check only for the sake of the children.

"What did you say?" Isabel repeated in a strained voice, as ash-gray as her husband.

"It's been three months, Mamá. I'm pregnant, there's nothing I can do about it."

The belt struck her right in the face, raising an ugly welt and splitting her lip. Her brothers scrambled under the bed to hide.

When her mother tried to separate them, she too felt the painful bite of the lash and couldn't keep the man from unleashing his rage on the girl's body.

The scene played out in silence, though. Nobody screamed or shouted this time. Zé found this silence even more terrifying, because she knew what it signified.

All that could be heard were the girl's soft whimpers, Gerardo's heavy breathing, the mother's restrained moans, and the crack of the belt as it sliced through the air and fell remorselessly across Zé's body.

The complicit silence during such scenes of torture and violence formed part of the history of daily life on That Island, like a form of Noh theater, in which painful pauses fill the viewer's mind with timeless and instructive plots.

Scenes like this abounded in the Havana of the seventies. Violence had to be performed backstage, in silence, and with dramatic perfection but without justice or consequences, with no moral to the story, as if they were taking place in the fearsome forest gloom of some bleak jungle where predation is the natural law.

Violence of any sort was always silent, there more than anywhere else. A man would kill a woman out of jealousy, and not a single mention of the unfortunate event would appear in the papers. A woman would douse her husband, a prominent athlete, with kerosene and burn him alive. Another woman would kill a famous boxer. And nothing. People would hear about it through what Cubans call "Radio Bemba," Radio Fatlips, what people elsewhere call the grapevine. Two women, the wife and the mistress, would take up knives to "ventilate" the wife's husband, the mistress's lover, and people would turn a blind eye. A father would kill his daughter with a baseball bat because she was pregnant with a best friend's baby (the father's best friend, that is), and—shush, quiet!

The silence was filled with deception and lies. They always lied (just as they always hid and manipulated data about diseases that the revolution had supposedly eradicated), because it seemed natural to them that such cases couldn't exist in this wonderful society of violent guerrillas, who nowadays we would call terrorists. Nothing of the sort could happen, because they had prevented such things, imposing obedience and obligatory silence. The explanation that would come later was that barbarities happened only under capitalism; but beyond that, for the great majority, what they considered to be their right—the right to kill, to torture, to inflict pain—constituted the regular, normal way. And they spread this sick habit, corrupting the life of an entire nation.

Thus the Cuban is such an easily influenced sort, so faithful to his enslaver genes that he instantly adopted the savage law of the jungle as the island was transformed into a gigantic plantation. The machete was the solution to every problem, or in its absence the knife, fire, poison, whatever was closest to hand. Acting violently even earned you some prestige. The more violent, the more macho you were. More points in your revolutionary dossier, more credits in your file; useful for scoring all sorts of idiotic trivialities. For example, a membership card in the Communist Party. Which was, to be sure, a chore to obtain, demanding sheer brute force and strict obeisance to the code of silence.

Silence, always silence, since silence was how you saved the savage from getting dirty hands or being marked for life. Because, as a character in a Jean-Pierre Melville film said, "Silence never betrayed anyone." Bah!

Zé tried to lift herself up off the floor, but every time she raised herself to her feet she immediately collapsed again. She was bleeding from her nose, her ears. Half-blinded, she could barely make out what looked like shadows moving about her in slow motion. Her eyes were so swollen they looked like two festering slits. She held her hands across her belly to protect it when her enraged father, out of control, his eyes bloodshot, began kicking her there, hoping to kill first the fetus and then her, or so he muttered.

Isabel finally threw herself on top of her daughter to protect her, and the lashes of the belt again bit into her back.

The kids didn't cry. Children on That Island are tamed, broken like timorous little beasts of burden, trained, or rather domesticated, from the cradle. Scenes like this teach them from an early age that the best thing to do is to keep their mouths shut. At most they whimpered quietly while hiding under their cots.

Isabel managed to drag herself to the door with Zé crawling on all fours under her. She tried several times to open the latch, but Gerardo kicked her until he broke her forearm. At last Zé jumped up and yanked the door open, scraping the skin from her fingers on the lock. She rammed the latch back with unexpected rapidity, then ran out with her mother through the narrow opening they'd made, all while still wrestling with Gerardo.

The women's escape paralyzed the brute, who always avoided scandals from the door of his home on out, taking care not to let the neighbors find out and possibly report him, since a report might put his eagerly anticipated Party membership at risk.

The neighbors had heard the fracas, of course. But silence ruled their lives, too, and at this late hour they were pretending to be sound asleep so as not to get mixed up in anything that might prove socially damaging. The few lights that had still been on about an hour earlier when Zé got home had begun to turn off the moment the belt first ripped through the air and whimpers and groans were heard through the walls.

Isabel and Zé swept downstairs at full speed, not stopping for an instant. When they hit the street, they raced off, panting, in the direction of Calle Inquisidor. Halfway down the block, the mother came to a stop, completely out of breath.

"How could you do this to me, girl? How? How could you betray my trust?"

Zé was crying, moving her head from side to side. It hurt her to talk, her mouth was so badly beaten. All she could do was mumble, "Take me to Osiris's place, Mamá, please. I'll explain it all to you there."

"Osiris the whore? That Greek sailormen's whore? Why should I take you to such a disgusting creature's house?"

"Mamá, listen to me, Osiris is a good woman. Sure, she's a prostitute, but so what? She's the one who told me I should tell you the truth and that I should have my baby."

Isabel raised her arm and nearly slapped her, but she restrained herself. Lowering her hand, she wiped it angrily on the tattered skirt of her dress.

"That's the great advice she gave you? Did I raise you to take advice from whores? Come on, hurry! Let's get away before your father comes down and catches us!"

They walked uneasily down Calle Sol to San Ignacio. Crickets were chirping and fireflies flashing on the walls of the courtyard in the tenement where Osiris lived. The canopy of a thick-trunked ceiba, which had inexplicably sprouted from the center of the cement floor, towered over everything. They climbed the narrow spiral staircase and rapped on a half-open door. From inside came a woman's voice, the voice of an inveterate smoker.

"Come on in, whoever it is. It's too hot, so I left the door open. But you should know I'm not taking any customers today, I'm not going to work for anyone, not even Baudelaire if he appeared here naked and with his tongue hanging out. I'm reading *Sentimental Education*, by Flobert" (she meant Flaubert), "and I'm up to the end. Today's my reading day, because man does not live by ephemeral things alone. And . . . What happened to you, girl?" Osiris froze at the pitiful sight of the two bloodied, fearful, still skittish women now crossing the threshold of her ramshackle door. The cigarette fell from her lips.

Dark-skinned, her wavy hair neatly combed and cascading over her round, scented shoulders, with olive-colored eyes and fleshy lips, the woman had until that moment been lounging comfortably on a sort of Louis XV–style couch, like a divan, its hard cushion upholstered in passion red. She herself always referred to the divan by the classical term "triclinium," and she did so the moment they entered. "Allow me to descend from my triclinium and take a closer look at the two of you." She rose, sighed, snatched the cigarette butt from the floor, and ground it into an ashtray of Carrara marble.

She must have been roasting in the mid-August heat, what with lying on a couch covered in velvet and fake silk woolen pillows; *not the thing to do, couldn't be comfortable*, thought Isabel as for the first time she took a look around that hovel with airs of an Oriental palace. She surveyed the porcelain knickknacks, most of them broken, stuck back together with shoemaker's glue, then fixed yet again. She stared at the slipshod decorations, the trinkets piled up on an improvised dressing table, a plaster reproduction of the Venus de Milo. Life-size. The statue's head touched the ceiling, holding it up. Isabel did a double take and smiled sarcastically.

"The Venus is shoring it up for me, see the crack? The ceiling's falling down, and a friend gave me the statue to prop up the rotten beam. He stole it off the set of a cabaret on a cruise ship. A Greek ship, of course," she pointed out. "They were using it as a decoration, for publicity." She looked sidelong at Zé. "Well, I see you took my advice and told your parents what's up. I said 'your parents,' plural, because I deduced from the sad shape you two are in that your father, that sweet fellow, also heard the news. And obviously wasn't too happy about it."

"Who is this woman to you, girl?" her horrified mother asked. The grimace on her face, with her broken arm held in place by her good hand, reflected the growing pain she felt.

"Osiris is my friend, Mamá."

"More than your friend, your spiritual adviser," the woman boasted.

"Your friend? Your *friend*? Your 'spiritual adviser,' she says? Your father was right, so right! You're crazy, out of your mind—or shameless, thoughtless, sick! This is such a dishonor for the family, sweet heaven! I need you to explain this whole business to me, Zé. But not here, not here! Let's go!" She tried to drag her daughter out, but pain shot up her arm, and she had to lean against the wall to deal with the dizziness that engulfed her.

Isabel wept with remorse, but quietly, softly, to keep Osiris's neighbors from finding out that she had visited such a place of perversion and disrepute, the hovel of this . . . loose woman, this prostitute, this . . . Greek sailor's whore!

Osiris offered her a leopard-skin armchair. Isabel agreed to sit, but on the very edge, to show that she had scruples. The hostess served them cold water from an ancient, luxurious American Frigidaire, in a pair of flowery glasses bought at the La Mina hardware store. Isabel gulped it down, hiccupping.

Next Osiris splinted Isabel's arm as best she could, washed and treated Zé's wounds with bits of cotton gauze and whatever medicine she had left in her cabinet, then did the same for the mother's wounds. She handed each a nightgown of hers, inviting them to sleep in the nook that she called her loft.

Turning to Isabel, she said, "Tomorrow you should go to the emergency room to get a proper cast put on that arm. I did what I could, but it's not good enough, and who knows if the bone won't set wrong. I don't know why the hell they closed all the emergency rooms in this country at night, I mean, like there aren't any nighttime accidents, murders, unexpected deaths, women with arms broken by the savages they picked to marry. 'Anyway, the sea,' as the poet Nicolás Guillén put it. Who is, by the way, a regular in this love attic. My house isn't fancy, but you'll be safe here," she insisted. Seeing how Isabel was eyeing the nightgowns, she added, "They're colorful, sure, but they're all I can offer. You've already figured out that I'm a Greek sailor's whore, not one of those boring Bulgarian pianists that get invited to this country, the ones they dress up so horrendously in those parrot-green togas that look like they might fly from the cage at any minute. You can rest here calmly, nobody will bother you."

"Right, this is the only place where my husband won't look for us," Isabel admitted.

"Don't be so sure, don't be so sure," Osiris replied sarcastically, then returned to the conversation with her air of a diva past her prime. "You'll sleep in my bed," she said, pointing at Zé, "and your mother on my triclinium, which is rather firmer." She let the word "triclinium" roll off her tongue in a distinguished accent.

"My daughter, a fine young lady, will never sleep in a Greek whore's bed!" Isabel muttered in fury.

"Isabel—let me call you by your first name, though you aren't my friend, and I don't think you ever could be, and I've known that for some time, and to top it off you couldn't even imagine why you aren't or why you can't be. Look here, darling, your daughter isn't a 'fine young lady' anymore, if you've been paying attention. She's pregnant. Very pregnant. What's worse, pregnant by a Greek, and a merchant marine sailor at that. Or a soon-to-be sailor. In other words, she's nearly a whore herself. But she isn't a whore like me; I charge good money, and am proud to do it. Oh, and for your information, your daughter has already slept in this bed more often than you'd be able to stop her from doing at this point. In fact, she's not the only member of your family who's done that, if you catch my meaning. Poor Greeks! What good did it do them to be the fathers of Western civilization, the arts, culture! In this country, being a Greek sailor's whore is a calamity, a disaster, the worst thing that could happen! A Greek merchant marine sailor and a Greek are basically the same thing, if we think about it. Those Greeks are so despised, they have such a bad reputation—and a woman who's a Greek's whore? Forget about it! That's like saying she's got a life sentence, or that she's dying from some uncurable disease! The weird thing is that some women in this strange country are whores to potential criminals, and they don't even realize it."

Isabel stared at her, eyes popping, in shock. She knew that her husband had been unfaithful to her, but not this far, not so far as to go to bed with a Greek's whore. But better not to talk about that right now.

"Oh, my god! What the hell is this woman talking about? Is it true? Pregnant, by a Greek? Now your father is really going to die! You'll kill your father! But by all the gods, how did it happen? What was I doing that I didn't see, didn't notice something so horrid was happening? It's my fault, all my fault!" Isabel writhed on the floor, crawled up onto the divan, where she squeezed herself even more into a ball, in her grief and distress.

"Well, girl, better you should kill him with the truth than he beats you to death—the truth's always more comforting, isn't it?" Osiris said in an ironic tone, with a wink to Zé.

Zé knelt before her visibly despairing mother and took her hands into her own. Then, holding her mother's chin, she forced her to look her in straight in the face, or straight in the inflamed mass of flesh into which her father had transformed her cheeks, forehead, chin, mouth, eyelids, nose. She let it all spill out.

"Mamá, please. None of this is your fault. You aren't to blame for what I did. But besides, I didn't do anything wrong. I met Orestes by chance. Both of us were going to Regla, on the ferry, and I struck up a conversation with him. It was me, it wasn't even him going after me. He's the only child of a ship's captain. That Greek boat that ran aground in the bay a few months ago."

"In Emilio Salgari's novels they call kids like Orestes 'cabin boys,'" Osiris joined in.

"You mean to tell me that the Greek who dishonored our lives by making a baby with you—a baby that'll have who knows what sort of defects, if it's ever even born—that he's not even a sailor? Just a cabin boy? A nobody?" Isabel rolled her eyes toward heaven and noticed a lamp hanging from the ceiling that looked very similar to the one her husband had given her for her birthday. Exactly the same one, in fact; she was sure of it.

Osiris couldn't fail to notice. "It comes from the same place," she whispered, running the tip of her tongue across her upper lip.

"What does?" Isabel turned a rude stare on her.

"The sun, I mean," she rasped mockingly. "The sun that gives light to Greece comes from the same place. What I mean is that it's the same sun that lights a Greek sailor's way or a cabin boy's, it's the same sun that gives us all light. We shouldn't make a big deal about unimportant things! Besides, in a few months the kid will be a sailor, he'll have the higher rank, and that's that."

"Does the damn Greek cabin boy know how he's covered us in mud, abandoning you in this state?" her mother asked.

Zé shook her head.

"He doesn't know either? So what are we supposed to do? How are we going to fix this situation with your father? Because we'll have to find some way to fix it! It's not right, it's unfair! Your father'll make that kid come back, he'll make him marry you, immediately!"

Osiris planted herself in front of Isabel.

"Look. The first thing you have to do is calm those frayed nerves of yours, because you're starting to get to me. Then try to understand that—here's the real problem. It isn't about what your husband says or does. The real problem is that the Greek kid lives a long, long way from here. And even though I have his father's address—because he's one of my faithful clients and I'm planning to write to him and bring him up to date on what's happening; he'll have to wait for the letter to arrive, if the authorities don't intercept it—I don't think this will get solved the way you two seem to hope it will. Greeks really are 'sailors,' and they really are Greek, and I imagine you've heard the thing about 'a sweetheart in every port.' Besides, in this country it'll be almost impossible to marry her off to a Greek, or to any foreigner—even more impossible now, the times being what they are. And the way her belly will be growing, it isn't like any Cuban boy is going to marry her! On top of that, you know how long a letter takes to get from Havana to Matanzas, so tell me how long it'll take to Athens? That is, if the letter isn't, like I said, stolen before it gets there."

"So how are we supposed to fix this problem, by all the gods on Olympus?" Isabel touched her arm; the pain was unbearable.

"Ah, so I see you're becoming familiar with the ancestral gods and symbols of your son-in-law's family. At some other time you might have mentioned Oshún or Yemayá, but now you're clinging to the gods on Olympus. How quickly we adapt!"

Isabel clicked her tongue. "It's just a phrase. Do you have something for the pain?"

"The 'Greek's whore' might have one pill left in her medicine cabinet. In fact, it was one of those sailors who gave it to me," Osiris noted with irony. "Good thing you've started to tell the difference between true pain and a passing ache and are starting to put the real pain first." She went off and returned with a pill and another glass of cold water.

"Do you realize what we'll be exposing ourselves to when people find out you're pregnant? And having a Greek merchant marine sailor's baby! I mean, a cabin boy's, just a cabin boy's, on top of everything!"

"There's nothing to be done about her being pregnant, everybody'll figure that out soon enough. She should accept it bravely, as I've taught her to do. Being a woman means having to arm yourself with courage for any conflict that might come along; being a prostitute means being in constant conflict with everything around you, and I've made myself a strategist. As for the fact that the father is Greek, in other words a foreigner, there's no reason why anybody needs to know."

But in the tenements of Havana, the walls don't just have ears, they have snooping, creepy, elephant-sized ears, and even in the home of a slightly snobby Hellenic whore who lines her walls with corkboard—much as Marcel Proust did in the bedroom on Boulevard Haussmann in Paris where he ended his days finishing *In Search of Lost Time*—informers have managed to plant microphones. That was something not even Osiris knew.

"And who's to tell me you aren't a snitch and aren't working as an informer for the political police?" Isabel challenged her with eyes on fire. "Nobody in this country becomes a Greek's whore unless something bad happened to them."

"So who told you nothing terrible has happened to me? But let's leave that be, better for us. It's true, I have an arrangement with a special agent. I get Greek goods for him—cigarettes, clothes, shoes for his kids—and he leaves me more or less alone with my business. But I'm not a snitch, and I'll never be a snitch. I'll never work for the political police. I might be a whore, but I have my patriotic dignity."

"Patriotic dignity, patriotic dignity, what a way of talking out of where the sun don't shine. How did you find your way to this house?" Isabel turned to Zé, pretending to ignore everything else Osiris had said.

The prostitute answered for Zé. "Easy. The boy brought her here. Following in his father's footsteps, of course. His parents are divorced, so Orestes was able to come here with his father that time. The only model he has for how to behave is his old man, because his mother is half crazy, a hopeless drug addict. When I saw how in love they were, I thought, instead of them lying together out there under some dirty bridge or in some disgusting park, or him laying his hands on your daughter in a movie theater full of lice and crabs, well, I thought it would be better to lend them my bed, which I'm sure is cleaner than yours—and I know what I'm talking about, because I'm an expert in every sort of sweat, emanation, and effluvium."

Isabel recalled the tart, penetrating odor that Gerardo came back with every time he returned from his increasingly frequent "volunteer labor" trips.

"But what are we supposed to do, then? What can we do with the Armageddon that's headed our way?" Once more she collapsed.

"You have no reason to tell Gerardo the baby's father is still an insignificant cabin boy, much less that he's Greek. He shouldn't find out, at least not for now. Telling him would make matters worse."

"You know my husband?" Isabel asked after hearing his name fall so familiarly from the lips of this hussy. She suspected she was taking a big risk.

"Better than you can imagine," Osiris rasped richly, with a sideward glance at Zé. "I became acquainted with him through your daughter, of course."

"That isn't really knowing him. You'd have to live with him, day after day, put up with him, smell his farts, get used to his bad breath, put up with his shouting and his insults, accept his blows to your head like you were accepting a diamond tiara, and despite all that still love him and go to bed with him, so that, in the end . . ." She paused, looking sidelong at her daughter. Osiris went on for her:

"So that in the end you figure out that you've been acting like a slave, like an idiot, for no reason, and getting so little in return. Yesssss, I do know about all that, too. I've lived through it in the flesh. That's one of the reasons why I practice the world's oldest profession. I dominate men, they don't dominate me. They come looking for me, I don't go after them. I don't have to love them or keep any sort of commitment. I always get along great with them, their money, and their desires. Though the older I get, the more philosophical I become. Sometimes I care more about their desire than their money, because I naturally find their desire for me flattering. Vanity lasts longer and purifies you better than money, which I throw away on all sorts of nonsense."

"Don't listen to her. Whatever has to happen to a woman is going to happen. It's always more rewarding for a woman to be a mother and a wife than to be a slut—a Greek's whore!"

"A wife, a wife! I can already see the photo of the happy event, fists bound and the whole *manengue*! Ball-and-chained to a cruel, useless idiot. As for being a mother—do you really think a whore like me doesn't have a right to be a mother, Isabel? You think we aren't mothers? Look, open your ears, listen close: I had two boys. One died. My mother-in-law took the other from me. One of my mothers-in-law. But what had to happen happened, and here I am. From mother to courtesan, to avoid the word that's so hard on your ears. From mother to whore! Or motherfucker, as the Spaniards like to say, those brutes."

Zé saw tears in Osiris's eyes and a bitter frown that had never darkened her face before.

"Look, let's drop this subject, we shouldn't let ourselves get sidetracked," her mother whispered dolefully.

"Yeah, we'd better get back to what's important to you—and not what's important for your daughter, huh?"

"One question strikes me." Isabel shook her head, as if trying to dislodge Osiris's words, which felt more and more intimidating. "What language did you and Orestes talk in? How can you fall in love with a man you can't understand?"

"We spoke Spanish, and he was starting to teach me some Greek," the girl replied timidly.

"Bah! As if speaking the same language would help us understand some of those beasts. What difference does it make, neighbor? They communicated in the language of love, the language of caresses, touch, desire, the body, the language of feelings and emotions. When that happens, the words burst out all on their own, and you can understand everything, absolutely everything. But, listen, I can confirm that she's telling the truth. Both Orestes and his father speak Spanish well enough, and they're charming people. Anyway, I see it's getting late, and I think we should go to bed. By midday tomorrow I have to be working—that's what I call it, but it is work, no matter what. I can accompany you to the hospital if we leave very early, but I won't be able to stay there with you two."

"No, no thanks," Isabel quickly replied. "We can go by ourselves."

"Oh. You don't want to be seen with me. I understand. You're not the first."

"That's not it, Osiris, it's that it'll be awful if Gerardo catches us all there together," she faltered.

"Yeah, I can believe it—awful for him, though I suspect that the mere fact of seeing us all there together would calm him down. Whatever. Do what you two think is best, or best suits you."

She handed out clean sheets and opened a fold-up cot for herself, on which she also spread lavender-scented sheets.

"How do you get lavender?"

"A client from Marseilles. That's where he gets it to bring to me."

They lay down, and Osiris turned off the tenuous light of an orange-tinted lamp. From the darkness she suggested, "It would be best for you if you could spend your pregnancy in the countryside, so your child can be born far from the filthy, ideologizing swamp that Havana has become. I don't know if you have family in the countryside . . ."

"My sister lives in Matanzas. I used to send Zé to stay with her during vacations."

"And I get along great with Tía Adela, her library is amazing!" the young woman sighed.

"Ah, an intellectual," Osiris muttered, unenthusiastic.

"She's a teacher. Musicology is her specialty, and she used to travel often to Europe, before 1959. She reads a lot, collects books. But we'll be walking a fine line, because Gerardo can't stand her."

"If only she was a whore or something, I'd love her. Sorry, pardon me," she rasped again. "It's not a bad idea to send her to Matanzas for the time being. You know what they call Matanzas?"

"Yes, the Athens of Cuba," Isabel sighed.

"So Petros won't grow up far from his paternal roots." She suppressed a smile.

"Petros? Why Petros? I'll never name my son Petros," Zé protested.

"Of course he'll be called Petros, because it means 'little pebble,'" Osiris insisted.

Zé liked the idea of "little pebble."

"Petros isn't bad. It's like Pedro, but with class," her mother added in a slightly pedantic tone.

"And how are we going to explain to Papá that we're going to call the baby Petros, not Gerardo, like him? Won't he suspect that his father is Greek, from the name?"

"Oh, girl, your father's a fathead! Don't worry, I'll make up some story for him. No way that child will be named Gerardo! Not over my dead body! But why Petros, Osiris?" Isabel asked, curious.

"It's the name of the greatest love of my life. A Greek man, of course."

"A sailor?" mother and daughter asked in unison.

"Yes, naturally, but he wasn't only a merchant marine sailor—he was a revolutionary! Another revolutionary!"

All three broke out laughing.

"What do you want? Nobody's perfect!" More laughter. "Shhh, quiet! Caramba, we'll wake the neighbors, if we haven't already, a long time ago!"

After a bit more whispering, yawning, and stretching, they fell asleep, exhausted but happy. Osiris dreamed of Petros. Isabel, of Osiris. Zé dreamed of a certain round face with eyes the color of coffee. Greek coffee.

THE OFFICE WALLS of the bureaucrat who had called her in were painted a blinding white. The shiny aluminum Miami-style windows were hermetically sealed. The air conditioning was on full blast, so strong she felt the chill in her bones and began to tremble uncomfortably from head to toe as she sat in the straight-backed gray plastic chair.

His desk teemed with all types of random objects. An ashtray sporting the logo of the Industriales baseball team. A box of Montecristo Number 2 cigars. A snapshot of three teenagers dressed up like little Camilo Cienfuego-ses. Another of a fat, smiling woman who looked like the cat that swallowed the canary, a genuine vixen (must be his wife). Garishly colored pencils methodically arranged in a Havana Club Rum glass with their sharpened ends pointing to the ceiling. Piles of green folders. A small box filled with seashells. A heap of DVDs by local musicians, awards, medals, tiny flags from every country. Zé stared at the Greek flag, with its striking white and blue stripes.

She was so busy looking at everything around her, just passing the time, that she hardly noticed when the official who had called her in entered the room. Official or busi-nessman; in this case it amounted to the same thing.

The portly man held his hand out rudely for her to shake. Sprawling back in the wide rolling armchair with his desk between them, he turned his smile-like grimace on her, elbows on the mahogany, chin in hand. Then he pushed himself back, opening first one file cabinet, then another, acting like he was hunting for something in them. He searched through the papers on his desk, inside another pile of darker green folders, and at last returned his elbows to the desktop, eyes fixed on a file.

"Let's see," he said, pretending to read it with close attention. "Mm-hmm. Mm-hmm. So this is how things look: you also want to travel to Greece."

"As you know, my son has been invited on a trip, and he has invited me."

"So, who is your son?"

He already knew; he was well aware, he couldn't pretend not to know that her son was the most famous *música campesina* guitar player and songwriter on the island and abroad at that time.

"My son's name is Petros Loynaz Martínez."

"Petros. Petros Loynaz Martínez. Ah, to be sure. Indeed. Nobody's ever explained his very odd name to me. Is that his stage name?"

"No, it's his real name."

"Strange. He's the first Cuban I've heard of named Petros. Why didn't you name him Pedro?"

"Right, Petros is the same as Pedro, but a girlfriend gave me the idea of naming him Petros."

"A girlfriend? And why would you have christened your son with a name suggested by this girlfriend?"

"I was very young. . . ."

"Yes, I'm aware of that detail. I know you had your son when you were very young, underage, and against the wishes of your father—a fine man, a revolutionary, someone who sacrificed his political life and even his leadership career. Nearly lost his Party membership. All that being your fault."

"That's in the past. I'm forty-nine now. My father's a very old man. I don't consider myself guilty of anything. And my son wants me to accompany him on his tour of Greece. That's all."

"So, you had Petros when you were sixteen."

She nodded, blushing. The old method, once again. The interrogation and, of course, the silences. The less she said, the less she'd be risking, she thought.

"How's old Gerardo holding up?"

"He's fine, living with me and his grandson, my son."

"Here in Havana, according to what I'm told." He clasped his hands over his beer belly.

"Yes, we brought him to our house. His second wife died and he feels lonely and sick. His other children don't pay enough attention to him. My brothers check in on him only now and then."

"Those children he had with his second wife are serious people, revolutionaries. I've seen the evidence, I know them."

"I don't doubt it."

"And how about your mother—Isabel, your own

mother—and the other woman?" He interlaced his fingers, as if to imply they were somehow partners in crime.

"They're fine, thanks," she replied dryly. "The other woman is my Tía Adela. Or do you mean Osiris?"

"They're still in Matanzas, from what I see. . . ."

The fact that he used the plural, *they*, was the clue that the interrogation was getting to the most delicate part.

"Yes, my mother's still in Matanzas, living with her sister, my tía."

"With your aunt, and also with the other citizen, Osiris Díaz Álvarez. Profession: the world's oldest." He put rude emphasis on the last phrase.

"Osiris is her partner and an honest woman. She cleaned up her past, she's following the law."

"So, your mother abandoned her home. Abandoned, that is, an impeccable revolutionary to run away and live a romance, to put it elegantly, with no more and no less than a Greek's whore."

"Greece is our country's ally, and Greeks are on the left, for the most part, and they love the Cuban people," she recited by heart.

"Come on, come on, Zé Loynaz Martínez, drop the slogans, we know how you think. Actually, you have an odd name, too: Zé. You people sure have a thing for exotic names: first Petros, then Zé . . ."

"My father wanted to call me Zenaida, but my mother hated the name, so they christened me Zé, which my

mother liked but not my father. They could never agree.
All my brothers have common names. Gerardo, my father's
name, is kind of impossible too, isn't it?"

"No, not so much as yours; in fact, Gerardo is a normal
name, like every revolutionary's name. Yes, as for oddities, I
noted this earlier, your mother always fell for oddities, like
the odd whim of leaving your father for a whore and con-
verting to lesbianism overnight."

"My father used to beat my mother, he abused us all.
My mother met Osiris and discovered love. They fell in
love. Also, it's just *being lesbian*, not *lesbianism*. It isn't a
medical condition, like rheumatism. Some people are gay,
some are lesbian."

"Great, now we're starting in on the lectures. Let's get
back to the point. Zé, you're forty-nine now, and you've
never traveled abroad. You were married, and your husband
recently divorced you or left you for another woman. You
didn't have children with that man."

She shook her head no.

"Why not?"

"He couldn't have children. And he left me for other
women, not for one woman in particular. I was the one
who suggested the divorce."

"Did you love him?"

"Of course. He was a good substitute father for Petros
and he still cares about him, after his own fashion."

"But you left him—or did he leave you?"

"No, he left me. He wanted to live alone and be like you, a successful businessman, and live his life. Now that being a successful businessman is all the fashion in this country, he wanted to make money, too. In the end, I found out that he wasn't living alone. He was cheating on me—he'd hooked up with an old girlfriend, and later I found out he was also going around with a younger woman from Mexico."

"And who is the father of your son?"

She began trembling inwardly.

"I don't know, I never found out. I was raped by a bunch of boys when I was sixteen."

The man ran his thumb across the thick file, pretending to leaf through the pages, as if inspecting them, convinced that the woman he was questioning was hiding something from him.

"Let's see, Zé. . . . Isn't Petros's father a Greek? A sailor in the Greek merchant marine?"

Apparently, he was also convinced that it would always be more proper for a woman to be raped by a gang of undesirables than to fall in love with a Greek sailor.

"No, I can assure you, Captain. The police never caught the gang that raped me. I never heard that any of them were Greek. Their identities were never established."

"Listen here, Zé, let's leave my rank as a captain of State Security out of this. With you, right now, at this moment, I'm just the person organizing your son's world tour, and as you can imagine, I have to be informed about everything, know every last detail about you and your son, because at this stage in my life I can't afford the slightest slipup, and I'm not going to let some misstep shadow my professional career. You already ruined your father's life; I won't let you ruin mine."

"I'm telling you the truth, Captain. You know Osiris was tried and found guilty by a revolutionary tribunal, and on account of that she spent five years in prison. She was convicted of prostitution with Greeks; my father also accused her of corrupting my mother and me, and my mother and I both testified in her favor during that . . . trial." She was about to add the adjective *shameful*, but left it out. "Regardless, none of the authorities could ever prove the rape by the five teens, simply because they weren't interested in trying to find them. They were too blinded by the belief that I practiced prostitution, the same as Osiris. Which is a lie, as I'll insist to the day I die, because I told them nothing but the truth."

"Indeed. On the other hand, your father always suspected that your son was the child of a Greek, a sailor in the Greek merchant marine, and that Osiris had forced you into prostitution with your mother's consent."

"That's a disgusting lie, as I've always said. Anyway, all that's in the past. My father is old and not well, he adores his grandson, he's resigned himself to the fact that his life didn't turn out the way he'd wanted. None of the libels against Osiris or my mother could be proved. My mother is reaching old age, she lives with her partner, she scrupulously obeys the law. My tía owns the house where the three of them live, and where I also used to live. That's where Petros grew up."

"Yes, Isabel's sister, your aunt—a dangerous woman. A half-crazy intellectual." His tone had suddenly become very familiar.

"No. Well, yes, a half-crazy intellectual." She couldn't help smiling. "An eminent musicologist. I owe Petros's education to her more than anyone. Without her, Petros wouldn't be the musician he is today. Or without Osiris, either."

"Osiris? What does Osiris have to do with Petros and his music?"

She chose to remain silent.

"You refuse to answer?"

"She told him all about musical instruments—from all over the world." She swallowed hard.

"Of course. Greek musical instruments. She was the one who gave him a bouzouki, that little guitar thing—a ridiculous instrument."

"It was my aunt who gave him that," she lied.

"That's what you say. Let's see: Petros is very enthusiastic about this trip. He's a man who's been all over the world, yet this trip is the one that has him really excited. It's weird, because he's been a hit everywhere, but nothing has excited him more than this trip to Athens and Crete and being successful there."

"I can tell that you know Petros. When we first started talking, I thought you didn't know him. I think part of his enthusiasm over Greece must be my fault."

"In what sense? I do know him, of course, how could I not know who he is—he's one of the musicians who earns the most money for us. His fame pays off. Pays *us* off. In what sense are you responsible for this excitement?"

"I'm a literary critic. I gave him lots to read, especially ancient literature, the ancient Greeks. I graduated from the University of Matanzas. That's why he'd love to take me to see Greece—imagine, that's one of my lifelong dreams." She stopped talking, afraid her tongue was getting too loose.

"A dream, a dream. Everybody here thinks they have the right to dream. Today's world isn't fit for us to skip about from dream to dream, like a bunch of nomads or restless dreamers. Especially not in this country! In this country we can't afford the luxury of letting brains like yours wander around all over the place, getting filled with outlandish dreams."

She smiled. Still on about the same old crap. Half a century later, still droning on about it, she thought; it was like a sort of mantra, or a mask, handy for hiding your true intentions: knocking down your neighbor, crushing him.

"I'm afraid I don't think the way you do. The world needs dreamers, poets, now more than ever."

"Oh, poets. What a headache, poets. But let's leave this conversation for another day—I can see from your smile that you found my observation amusing."

A long silence followed, heavy for her, ruminant and cheerful for him.

She was about to get up to leave, interpreting the extended silence as a sign that her trip with Petros wouldn't be approved. But noticing her squirming uncomfortably in her chair, he jumped up before she could move and announced—once more in his formal tone, as if he were handing her a treasured national relic like Maceo's machete or something—"You may travel as part of our delegation. This office shall complete all necessary paperwork: passport, exit permit, visa. Of course, your son will have to pay for everything on your behalf, as well as cover your personal expenses. Ah, but what am I thinking? They've already told me he's agreed to do just that. Congratulations, comrade! Please give your father a hug from me and one from my aging father. My old man and I have the greatest respect for him; how terrible, a great man ruined all because of . . . Anyway, as you yourself say, that's all in the past. And in our present moment, the past can only cast a shadow on our road to the future. A future of new beginnings and business."

Zé still wore a frightened smile. She felt a strange desire to hug this stranger who had kept her in suspense for more than an hour, but she restrained herself and merely pressed the officer's coarse hand once more.

"Remember, Zé, I'm Captain Fandiñas to my close friends, to everyone else I'm Rodolfo, just another music manager. You've heard how we've reinvented ourselves for the capitalists, though we maintain our rebel attitude, which some find novel and even attractive. But don't forget: what we have here is and will always be communism. After all, socialism or death!" He thumped his straight index finger against the desktop.

Pardon the redundancy, she said to herself.

She left that oppressive office, situated in an elegant old mansion in Miramar. She walked aimlessly under the blazing sun in search of a bus stop that would take her as close as possible to Calle Muralla, where Petros had bought a kind of minor colonial palace and restored it. The two of them lived there, together with her father, and he had also built himself his own recording studio in it. The palace was none other than the old tenement where she and her brothers had spent part of their childhood in an atmosphere of stench and decay.

She fished in her bag for a pair of sunglasses and set them on her nose, then called Petros on her cell phone.

"Yes, Mamá, so what did they say?" he asked hopefully.

Behind his voice she heard the chords of the bouzouki, the folkloric pear-shaped Greek guitar, blending with the notes of the tres, the traditional Cuban *campesina* guitar, in a recording that was playing in the distant background.

"I can come with you, Petros! They're letting us travel together!" she blurted out happily.

"See? I told you they wouldn't turn you down."

"I'm very happy, son, so happy!"

"Me, too, Mamá. Don't take too long, you know, Abuelo keeps on coming down to the studio. He spends his whole day sticking his nose into everything, pressing every button on the mixer. He gives his opinions on stuff he doesn't knows anything about. Next time you'll have to leave him tied up, or I'll do it myself. He never stops screwing around."

"Same as he's always done, son, at that he's a champion. Your grandfather is a meddler, he can't help it. Didn't your uncle Miguel come by to pick him up?"

"He called to say he couldn't, like usual—maybe tomorrow, maybe the day after. You know how your brothers always skip out on their old man. I can understand, dealing with Abuelo isn't easy."

"I know, he never was. Don't worry, I'll be there soon. I mean, as soon as I can."

"Take a taxi, Mamá."

"I will if I can find one. See you soon. Have you two had lunch?"

"No, we'll wait for you. It's still early."

She put her phone away and stood in the middle of

the sidewalk, hesitant. She couldn't make up her mind whether to keep walking to the oceanfront avenue, where it was usually easier to catch a taxi, or stay where she was on Quinta Avenida in the hopes that one might pass by, which would be a rarity in that neighborhood full of cars with diplomatic license plates and the insignia of the Central Committee.

In the end, she decided to wait. It was too hot to walk another dozen blocks to the Malecón avenue, with the bus route that ran along the sea, or to the parallel street a block from it.

She'd been waiting no more than ten minutes when at last she glimpsed a silver car in the distance, a Mercedes-Benz; she was surprised to see the driver slowing down just as he passed her, then pulling over close to the sidewalk and parking just meters away. And then sticking his hand out the window to wave her over.

She could tell it wasn't a car for hire or a taxi. From the license plate it looked instead like it belonged to a joint venture, a part-private, part-state owned business. Zé approached, telling herself that maybe the driver was lost and wanted to ask for directions. Bending down by the empty front passenger seat to peer through the window at the driver, she recognized one of her son's friends, a classmate from primary school, high school, and even university.

"Hello, Zé, remember me?" The young man wore a goatee, and she had to squint to see past his new look.

"Of course, Isaías, I do remember you! How long it's been! Do you live around here? Or are you looking for an address?"

"No, no way, I don't live around here. I work for a foreign company a few blocks away. It's so good to see you! Maybe I could walk with you, or give you a lift?"

"I'm going home, to my house in Habana Vieja."

"Same direction I'm going! Please, get in." He leaned across to open the passenger door.

Zé got in, they kissed cheeks, and Isaías drove off.

"How you've grown, Isaías!" Zé commented.

"We've all grown. Petros is a real artist. He got superfamous with all that Greek and *campesina* music. And you're as beautiful as ever."

She smiled shyly at the unexpected compliment.

"Have you seen Petros lately?" she asked, still blushing.

"No, I hardly have time for anything. And he has even less, with all his practice sessions and concerts and tours. But we talk on the phone all the time. I just wish we could get together more often. I have such good memories of growing up together in Matanzas. Such great times! I remember how friendly everybody was in your house—you, Abuela Isabel, Señora Osiris, Tía Adela. Señora Osiris used to make us *anón* fruit ices while we went swimming in the tidal pool—in all that heat!"

Señora Osiris, Zé thought. *Señora Osiris*. Since when were people who'd been condemned by the system with barely so much as a trial, the way Osiris and so many other innocent women and men had been, given the titles of *Señora* or *Señor*? Only recently. Only since the gangsters who stole democracy on the island had decided to stop being rabid communists and had turned instead into savage capitalists.

While the young man spun pleasant memories, Zé listened with reserve, sometimes smiling, sometimes wistful, turning to look out the car window from time to time and contemplate the crowds shuffling like zombies through the streets of Havana—the people of Vedado, the people of Centro Habana, poorly dressed, weary. Dragging their feet and invariably carrying raggedy shopping bags, almost always empty.

". . . And then, well, we all got out of Matanzas and settled in Havana. I can't complain, things have gone well for me. For a guy from Matanzas, making it in this city is no game—you really gotta hustle!" He laughed out loud at his own boast.

"For a girl from Havana, on the other hand, getting used to Matanzas was pretty easy. Matanzas is a nice city, and from the cultural point of view it can hold its own against any other. Sometimes it even beats the capital. Matanzas is the cradle of so many poets and musicians. Petros was born in Matanzas, but I'm from Havana, don't forget. Or maybe you didn't know."

"No, I didn't. So why did you move to Matanzas, then?"

A tremendous rainstorm suddenly began to pour.

"I was sixteen, and I had to move away to please my parents. I don't regret it, Isaías, I don't regret anything. I was pregnant—with Petros—and back then that was really frowned on."

The young man had closed the car windows. The rain lashed at them. The wipers started sweeping rapidly back and forth across the windshield. Zé's gaze melted and ran together with the water as it dripped down the glass.

SHE MANAGED TO say goodbye to only one of her best friends at school, Yocandra, who was more or less aware of what had happened. Zé had told her that she was pregnant with the child of a foreigner, a young Greek named Orestes, and that she felt she was in love for the first time. But she didn't want to add that the young man was just a cabin boy, the son of a ship's captain, with an uncertain future in the merchant marine. No way.

She didn't get to say goodbye to her father, who refused to see her. Her mother wanted her to hug all her brothers before the two of them took the Hershey train to Matanzas. The farewell was short and sad.

Mother and daughter boarded at the small station across Havana Bay. The train was very old, loud, and slow. Blackish steam rose from the brakes, overheating the wooden floor. On top of the unbearable heat, there was the ozone from the shaky ancient overhead electrical connectors.

She was sweating buckets, dizzy, sick to her stomach.

"When will we get there, Mamá?"

"Soon, girl, soon."

No, not soon, not soon at all. Those nearly twelve hours were the most horrific of her life. Endless, when the trip shouldn't have taken more than six.

Two hours before they arrived at the station in Matanzas, unable to hold it in anymore, she threw up on the head of the passenger in front of her. There was a tremendous

45

uproar. The man jumped from his seat, infuriated, covered with clotted vomit, while everyone else began cursing and hurling coarse insults at her. Isabel quickly pulled out a clean towel and small bottle of alcohol and, while giving Zé the alcohol to smell, tried to clean up the poor passenger. But the people kept yelling that the girl was to blame.

"She's a pig!"

"Swine!"

"Shameless! She did it on purpose!"

"She's pregnant, damn it!" Isabel yelled at last. "And I know what I'm talking about—I'm her mother!"

After that they stopped shouting, but the mutters and grumbling continued.

Isabel's explanation had just made things worse. What? Pregnant, at her age? Who was the baby's father? And why wasn't he here with her? The comments and the rumors, just whispers at first, grew in volume from the first coach to the last until even the engineer in the ruin of a locomotive heard that a pregnant teenager was traveling in one of the cars, that you couldn't see her swollen belly yet, but she had thrown up on one of the passengers, that the baby's father wasn't there, wasn't accompanying her, nor did anyone know who he was, and that the only person by her side was a hysterical woman who claimed to be her mother.

The railway worker shrugged, indifferent. He had to give all his attention to the railway, which was in terrible condition: to whoever or whatever might wander distractedly onto the tracks—more likely drunks than cows at this point, now that there were hardly any cows left—to the morons who might jump the tracks and get cut in half. He had no time for all these fool passengers, always so hungry for gossip.

The engine gave a weary whistle at the end of its journey.

Tía Adela was there on the platform, waiting for them. So stylish, wearing a long skirt in four shades of green and red, tied at the waist with a wide brown leather belt, a white blouse with an embroidered front and three-quarter-length sleeves, hair gathered in a tall bun, feet shod in a pair of worn ballerina shoes. She hadn't aged, though she looked a little pale, and she now wore a pair of round gold horn-rimmed glasses she had inherited from her mother.

After everyone had hugged, good-hearted Adela stroked her niece's chin and announced to her, "I want you to know that I will support you in every way. I don't have the slightest idea what they did to you, or what you did, but I'm here for you. My house will be your house. Starting tomorrow, you can go to school here."

Zé smiled, thankful and relieved. Isabel cut her sister short.

"Don't make up your mind so quickly, Adelita," she corrected her, calling her by her childhood nickname. "We'll explain things when we get to your place. As for school, we'll have to see whether they'll accept her or not, with the condition she's in. We've had a terrible trip here, that train is a genuine calamity."

"The countryside looks beautiful from the train, doesn't it?" Adela said to lighten the mood, as the three of them headed for the exit to the station.

Zé carried a small suitcase, which weighed less than her mother's. Adela tried to help them, but neither would let her. Her hands were delicate even though she was used to working the land, but she was mainly devoted to music.

"Yes, the views out the window are lovely, but the riff-raff on the train don't let you appreciate them. You know how things go in this country. I understand now why you've never traveled since 1959. You don't even visit us in Havana."

"If I don't visit you in Havana, dear sister, it isn't because of the problems with the train. The reason is your husband, an unbearable person. I might even imagine that he's the one behind your daughter's temporary exile."

"Yes, I know, it's his fault, but the fact remains that riding that blessed train broke all my bones. Gerardo's getting worse and worse. He's obsessed with politics and moving up socially. He doesn't realize it, but that era ended quite a while ago, and the politicians we have now are all we're ever going to get. The ones who've been named to their positions, put in place by . . ." She flicked two fingers twice against her right shoulder in the common sign for the commander's epaulets. "Now he's gotten it into his head that they have to give him membership in the Communist Party. What a thing to get stuck on these days!"

"Who cares about him or what he thinks," Adela muttered. "We live life differently here, Zé. This is a province, not the capital. It isn't Havana. But the city of Matanzas has lots of history, and it's full of rivers and poets. And brilliant popular musicians. Here you'll become a woman, find a good man, study at the university, which is widely respected."

Isabel and Zé glanced at each other and smiled. They had so much to tell Tía Adela.

Her place wasn't far from the station, just eight blocks. It was a whole house, three stairs up from the street to the front door. A small entrance hall, four wide wooden rocking chairs and a center table to furnish the living room, a parlor room to one side, a corridor leading to an open courtyard filled with blooming flowerpots and the house's three bedrooms. The kitchen was in the back, next to a small dining room. Behind it was the bathroom, with a tub with bronze claw-feet—very old-fashioned but solid and clean. The parlor featured a piano.

Adela showed them around the house as if they were visiting for the first time, pointing out each of the repairs she had made since the last time they were there. That had been two years earlier. Zé remembered that her youngest brother had only just been born, and the family had gone to spend the summer vacation with their aunt. But then Gerardo and Adela stopped talking with each other because of a silly argument over their favorite baseball teams. Her father liked Industriales, the Havana team, while her aunt

rooted for Yumurinos, or the Matanzas Crocodiles, as the
people there called them. They stopped talking for months
over this disagreement. In the end Adela forgave him and
tried to avoid the topic whenever she and her brother-in-
law talked long-distance.

"This will be your bedroom, Zé, the second one. You
know I sleep in the first bedroom, to be near the front
door in case anyone knocks. And near the telephone on
the stand in the parlor, to have it closer to hand if someone
calls at night. Yours is bigger. It's the coolest room, since it
faces the courtyard—"

"The jasmine smells so beautiful, Tía!" the girl broke in.

"Those are night jasmines. I care for them like they're
made of pure gold. Those are the only night visitors allowed
in this house. As far as I'm concerned, there won't be any
others," Adela sighed.

"You never heard from Antonio again?" asked Isabel.

Adela didn't know what to do with her arms. At last
she crossed them, squeezing her waist and prominent bust
even more tightly.

"No. He left four months ago now, and I haven't heard
from him since. You know better than anyone how I loved
that man, the only man in my life. Anyway, let's change
the subject." The light went out of her eyes, which found
a neutral spot on the wall hung with potted ferns to stare
at. "So tell me, let me in on it. What happened, that they
chased you off to here?"

"Gerardo is very upset." Isabel swallowed hard, but she went on with resolve. "Zé is pregnant. The father's a young man. Gerardo wants to marry her off."

"Ah, I see." Adela observed the young woman, sitting on one corner of the bed; her mother sat on the other edge, while the aunt stood before them. "Let's go to the dining room. You've got to be thirsty. I'll give you some of the nice cold lemonade I made before I went to pick you up."

They left their bags in the bedroom and followed the aunt to the dining room. As they each drank a tall glass of iced lemonade, they took up the conversation again from where they'd left off.

"So do you want to get married, or not? Who's the boy?" Adela inquired breathlessly. "Didn't you think first about how you're too young to get into a mess like this? Don't you have enough trouble with your mother having to deal with your brute of a father?"

"We've already asked all that, Adela, and I have warned her about it myself, but . . ." Isabel began to sob.

Zé had never seen her mother so fragile. In front of her sister she turned to nothing—cream, smoke, like a little girl beaten down by the other's firm strength. Then Zé spoke up. "I can't get married, and I don't want to. He isn't here in Cuba; he left on a ship. He's Greek, the son of a sailor in the Greek merchant marine."

"Well, then, that's a nice little problem you've gotten yourself into."

"Are you listening, Adela? With a Greek!"

Adela looked at her sister in surprise. "You say that like he's some sort of criminal. He isn't. Or is he?"

"The women in Havana who sleep with Greek merchant marine sailors, all of them, without exception, are whores. They have an awful reputation, and you know it." Her mother blew her nose on a little handkerchief trimmed with a wide lace ribbon.

"Oh, well, you don't really see that here in Matanzas, we don't give it any importance. There are sailors and Greeks here, too, and we have this big, beautiful bay, and ships docking at the port. But we're more cultured than you are in Havana," Adela added with pride. "We know that Greeks can be merchant marine sailors and also great poets, great writers, philosophers. And all at the same time. They're the fathers of Western civilization, and the fact that I'm going to have a Greek nephew is naturally a tremendous honor for me. Let's toast to it!"

Isabel watched as her sister retrieved a bottle of red wine from the refrigerator and poured out two cups with alacrity and grace. "You can't drink, but your mother and I can," she observed as she filled the fine Baccarat crystal glasses.

"Where did you get that crystal? And the red wine?"

"A neighbor who left for the North gave me the crystal before they could inventory her things. I got the wine under the table. I only drink it on important occasions."

"So you never drink?"

"Of course I drink! Every moment I exist is an important occasion. So you got here right on time, just before I ran out."

"Adela, don't you understand what a problem we're facing?" Isabel looked her straight in the eyes.

"Yes, I do. Raising a child is very complicated in this country, but we'll deal with it, the two of us." She pointed at her niece, then at herself. "You can come see him whenever you wish. This is your house."

"He won't have a father, Adela. You realize how the poor child is going to suffer on that account?"

"He'll have a mother, a grandmother, and an aunt. Besides, Zé will find someone, a good man, or who knows but the Greek might come back some day."

"And if he doesn't?" Isabel asked, bewildered.

"Mamá, I can do it myself, with Tía's help. If you've managed, why can't I? Besides, if having a father means having one like mine, better not to have one."

Isabel glared at her. "He's the one you have, the one I gave you. I know you're blaming me, but without him you wouldn't even exist."

"Great explanation, Isabel. Please!" Adela shook her head disapprovingly.

Isabel went back to inconsolable weeping. Her sister swept her tenderly into her arms. Only then did her moans soften.

That night and the next her mother stayed with them. But Isabel had to go back to Havana; the children had stayed behind with their father and a sister of his, and she was afraid he would vent his anger on them as he often did when she was away from home.

Zé saw her mother off, sure that she'd see her again in two weeks. But Isabel wasn't able to get back until two months later. Gerardo had forbidden her to have any contact with her daughter, threatening to report her if she abandoned the children again.

As soon as her mother left on the Hershey train, Tía Adela decided that they'd go the following morning to get Zé enrolled in the local high school. The director was a good friend of hers and the school she ran had already dealt with cases of pregnant young women from the countryside, who were never expelled or made to feel embarrassed for what had happened to them.

Indeed, the director didn't see it as an impediment, though she did ask with concern whether the young woman would be able to count on the baby's father. Adela felt obliged to say she wouldn't.

"She was . . . raped, in Havana, by a bunch of fellow students. It's a case that got hushed up, it was so horrific. It's very painful," she lied, just as she and her niece had agreed to do, to avoid going into any details about the Greek cabin boy, which would only complicate matters.

"Oh, poor girl." The director threw her a kindly gaze, as

she might have done for a dying patient, then immediately reverted to her normal expression. "Anyway, at least you survived."

She gave her the enrollment form on the spot and told her to come back to school the following day. Her belly still wasn't visible, so she could pass as a normal girl who had simply moved from the capital to the provinces.

During her pregnancy, her mother could manage to come see her only every other month. Gerardo never visited, nor did he agree to meet his grandson when he was born.

My dear friend Yocandra,

Today, April 22, Petros turns five. He's a very smart boy, he loves music, and he's been studying piano with my Tía Adela since he was three. I'd tell you he's a virtuoso if I didn't think you'd take me for a doting mother who's crazy about her baby. There's a little of that, what can I do? Petros can play Chopin and Debussy with a degree of pia-no-playing skill and an emotional depth that are incredible for his age, in the same way he plays Ernesto Lecuona, who you know isn't treated like a saint by the people in power, though they listen to him in private before trashing him in public.

Petros is a little boy like any other, he plays ball, he runs off to hang out with the guaguancó dancers who live in the nastiest tenements in the neighborhood, where he plays rumba de cajón on the tres. His playing is a huge hit. And, speaking of guitars, Osiris gave him this little one that he treats like a treasure. It belonged to one of her old Greek customers, her Petros, her revolutionary lover, whose name my son inherited. My mother was able to rescue that little guitar, a bouzouki, before they tore apart Osiris's home.

She's about to get out of prison. Her trial, as you know, was a real tragedy, shameful, held after they dragged her by the hair from the tenement room where she had set up her Hellenistic brothel, dragged her from her misnamed "triclinium" to Parque Habana. There they beat her, stoned her, humiliated her in every way. Which you'll remember, as you were a witness. I couldn't be, I was already living in Matanzas, but my mother told me all the details.

They held the people's court without delay in the center of the park, amid shouting and physical attacks. They handed down a five-year sentence for her after accusing her of prostitution—not just practicing it herself but also tricking teenagers like me into prostituting ourselves just as she had done—and, of course, of spreading counterrevolutionary propaganda, which was false. I have to reach a catharsis, I'm sorry, that's why I'm writing about something you saw with your own eyes.

My written testimony supporting her was dismissed as worthless, as was my mother's, who would also have been found guilty as a lesbian if my father hadn't used his prestige as a union leader to protect her. My father, who behaved so despicably toward both of them, still wanted to save my mother so he could keep being the kind of father he was: a beater, an abuser, a brute. But on the other hand, he ruined Osiris forever. My mother couldn't forgive him, and she never wanted so much as to hear about him after that. I hope this will change someday, which will happen when this country becomes different and all the hate quiets down.

Yes, I know you'll say that those were terrible times, that even though other things still happen, we don't have to put up with the violence we endured in those years.

That does nothing to relieve our past suffering or to erase Osiris's personal sacrifice, which will never fade from everyone's memories. Fortunately, she's had my mother's support, Adela's, my own; because, as you can imagine, they haven't done anything bad to my mother, since she's always been more or less watched over and favored from afar by the powers that shelter my father.

And to think that all those two women did was give themselves over sincerely to the love they felt for each other, loving each other for several nights in a row, in the intimacy of a tenement room, where supposedly nobody should have heard anything, nobody should have discovered their moans of pleasure. When they were denounced I was already living here with Tía Adela. As you can imagine, I hadn't heard about how they had become good friends or that they had secretly become lovers. Furtive lovers, who've paid dearly. Far too dearly.

Osiris wasn't the only one deeply injured by the outcome of the trial. My mother lost custody of my brothers, and she hasn't been able to get a job anywhere since then. Luckily, she can make a living by sewing clothes for the public. My brothers were given scholarships to schools far from her, to keep them away from her "bad example," according to the authorities. My father also moved far away, and, as you know, he rebuilt his life.

I admire my mother, who has remained faithful, waiting five years, putting up with everything, slings and arrows, and still hasn't let a day go by without visiting Osiris in that hideous women's prison, Manto Negro. "Black Cloak." Whose idea was it to give a prison a name like that? No, and not satisfied with that horror, they later transferred her to Nuevo Amanecer, "New Dawn," another fine name for a prison. These people are very witty when it comes to naming the most horrendous places. Adela, Petros, and I have gone to visit her there. They've never let Petros in, but at least she heard about the times Petros came. But he had to wait outside, holding the hand of one of the female wardens, until the half-hour visit they allowed my mother and me was over. Such a long trip for them to give us just half an hour.

I could send you a whole album of the drawings that Petros made when we'd get back from Nuevo Amanecer. He would imagine Tía Osiris's face behind bars, and always with a little guitar and hundreds of butterflies fluttering over her head, which he said were flying dreams. Well, look, without knowing it, Osiris had kept that bouzouki, which had belonged to her great Greek love. I know, all this is a little too cute, but isn't that life? Isn't life in this country a ridiculous telenovela, not a novel like Marcel Proust would have written? Anyone here who aspires to be the next Thomas Mann and write the next *Magic Mountain* ends up writing something that sounds more like *Burro Hill*. That's as high as you can go in this place.

Dear Yocandra, it's been so long since we saw each

other, so I wanted to recall all this with you. We can't forget any of the things that have been done with impunity in this country. But I especially wanted to write you to tell you about the latest details. Since the last time I had you here visiting a year ago, nothing has changed. I'm still the same university student with her little boy. People see me as more normal every day. Though nobody ever looked at me like I was an oddity, the way they would have seen me in Havana, even with contempt. People from Matanzas don't get all high and mighty, and they don't look down on you.

I love Havana, as you know; it's the city of my childhood, it's where I was born. But I also love this city deeply. Culture just flows everywhere here, without any fuss or affectation, and it's so natural. Being cultured and educated is just how people behave. There's a hidden culture that lives here, coming from the city's old poets, from its rivers, from its bay, from the young people with their mysterious spiritual strength, from its traditional music, from its legendary women, so elegant and sensual, from its men, so romantic.

I met a poet when I was leaving Teatro Sauto. Her name is Carilda Oliver Labra. She talked to me about another poet, who had been her husband, Hugo Ania Mercier. She invited me to her house. I was there with Petros for two hours, she reading me her poems until very late. When I got home I found out that Tía Adela had been worried I was gone for so long, but when I told her I had been visiting with Carilda it made her very happy, because they are great friends.

Hugo Ania Mercier was a distant relative of ours. Almost everyone in Matanzas is related to everyone else, you know, through close kin ties.

Hugo died in 1976 after his separation from Carilda, because he couldn't bear their breakup, they say, and committed suicide. Carilda wrote a poem dedicated to Hugo after he died, "In Place of a Teardrop." It's one of the most beautiful poems I've ever read. "You're far away now, a memory—no, impossible, you're safe in the glory of the poem. Hugo Ania Mercier: how I did love you."

It's not easy to find Carilda's poetry on the bookstands these day—not sure if you catch my drift—but I promise I'll send you a book signed by her. And a book by Hugo Ania Mercier, too, if I can find one.

I hope you'll be able to get back to this city that you were so passionate about, and where you also stirred a few passions. Yes, because you drove some of the boys in my department crazy, and one in particular who I'm sure you'll remember. Me, for my part, though I've caused a few stirs myself, I still can't get interested in anyone. The memory of Orestes still lives within me. Not quite as intensely as it used to, but I haven't been able to forget him, much less replace him. Nobody else interests me, because I just devote myself to taking care of my son, to my studies, and to my folks.

I'm just finishing up my next-to-last year of college. I would hate to spoil any of this, and above all I'd love to teach my father a good lesson. Not that he'd ever care about anything I did. Still, I know he finds out about absolutely everything we do, from A to Z, my mother, Petros, and I.

To make sure he doesn't think I've forgotten him, I sent him a photo of Petros with his bouzouki. Not simply to annoy him, but so he'll feel our presence. I hope he's discovered that the musical instrument his grandson is holding so lovingly in his hands is a Greek guitar, and I hope that drives him right up the wall. Just imagining that makes me laugh out loud.

Yocandra, how is life with The Traitor treating you? Not as well as you'd hoped, I suppose, but I know how much you love him and that you won't leave him for anything or anyone, and also that it won't be easy for you to free yourself from him. Does he love you in the same way, as you deserve?

I'm sending all my love, folded into this envelope, and a photo of me with Petros. Love.

Zé scrawled her signature, folded the newly finished letter, slid it along with a photo of herself and her little one into a stamped envelope. She sat for a moment in thought. As she gazed out at the row of hills covered in tall palms that spread into the impenetrable distance of the landscape beyond Matanzas, she told herself that one day she'd return to Havana, renounce her forced exile, and go for strolls again with Yocandra and her girlfriends, retracing the streets of her childhood.

She changed clothes, planning to run to the post office. On the way there she asked herself the same question she had been asking for more than five years. Would she ever see Orestes again? What had been going on in his life during those years? The young Greek cabin boy was probably already a merchant marine sailor who couldn't even imagine that a child and an eternal lover awaited him on that island in the Caribbean. Without realizing it, all these years she'd been harboring the hope of meeting him again.

THE OLD MAN sat in a corner fanning himself. It was an automatic, mechanical gesture; the temperature inside the air-conditioned recording studio was, in fact, rather cool in comparison to the heat outside.

Petros was pushing buttons again as he polished the sound of the music he'd just finished recording. Everyone was very happy with the result, and the crew members were taking their leave of the young man, who stayed behind with his Abuelo Gerardo.

"When does your mother get back? She always takes her own sweet time when she goes out. Always the slow-poke. Did the same to me when she was a teenager, always knocking around and shooting the breeze. And thanks to one of those times she stayed out late, just hanging around having fun, you were born. It was our fault too, of course, your abuela and me, we got careless. It went from knocking around to getting knocked up."

Petros pulled off his headphones.

"What were you saying, Abuelo?"

"Nothing, don't mind me, I was asking when your mother gets back."

"Soon, she'll be back soon. She called, Isaías is driving her back in his car. She phoned a while back to tell me."

"Who's this Isaías?"

"A friend of mine from childhood, Abuelo. We went to school together in Matanzas."

"Right, where they made you a musician."

Petros turned his back and started putting away the cables and other recording equipment.

He was young, tall, dark tan, with olive eyes and a tender gaze under eyebrows as thick and black as his hair. Fleshy lips, thick neck, strong wrists and arms, hands that were large but refined; muscular thighs squeezed into stone-washed jeans, sandals on his feet.

"Abuelo, why don't you read something? Don't you get bored hanging out with me?"

"No, my grandson, I like to see you working. And when will your mother be here? I'm hungry."

"Mamá left lunch made for us, I'll serve you. Let's go to the dining room, come with me," his grandson said solicitously.

The old man followed Petros to the dining table, pulled out a chair and sat down. Petros warmed the rice, fried some eggs, made an avocado and onion salad, and when the meal was ready, he set the steaming dish before his grandfather, with utensils and a clean napkin.

"What am I supposed to do when you two aren't here? So they gave your mother the OK to travel, too . . . What do I do with myself?"

"You'll stay with Tío Miguel."

"I don't like staying with Miguel. I can't stand his wife, she's such a gossip."

"But there's nothing you can do about it, there aren't any alternatives."

"And what does your mother want to go with you for?"

"You know, she wants to see Greece, and I can give her that pleasure, since this is the right time."

"Yes, you're half Greek, everybody knows—"

"Eating so early, Papá?" Her voice rang out from the entrance.

Zé was watching them from just inside the door. She came in, taking her bag down from her shoulder, house keys in her hand. Isaías came in behind her; he went over to give Petros a hug, then the old man, who barely paid him any attention.

"I ate breakfast early, I was hungry. You were late getting back again."

Zé gave her son a conspiratorial wink.

"Good thing, then, that you can get breakfast, lunch, and dinner in this house," Isaías said with a smile. "In my house, too. We're privileged people."

Petros ran off to grab a couple of beers from the refrigerator. Gerardo pointed a menacing finger at Isaías.

"Listen, you, I don't know who you are, but in this house we don't bad-mouth the government. Why do you have to go to Greece?" Gerardo asked his daughter.

"An old dream, you know that," she replied. "This is Isaías, a friend of ours."

"I don't care. No matter how long you look for that Greek sailor who got you pregnant, you're never going to find him."

A short silence.

"I won't be looking for anyone, Papá. I'll be there with

Petros, getting to see the country that I've learned so much about in my career."

"Bah, nonsense! More of your bullshit," the old man insisted. "You're going there for your own thing. What you should be doing is making up with your husband."

Petros interrupted. "Abuelo, finish eating and change the subject. Don't you see that you've been going on about the same old stuff your whole life? That playlist has gotten boring."

Zé signaled to her son to drop it, to ignore him. So Isaías and Petros went next door to the dining room to talk about their respective jobs and the hustle-bustle of being young.

"Why are you so difficult with men? You shouldn't be alone."

"They've been difficult with me, Papá. Why were you so damn hard on Mamá and me? Did you ever ask yourself that?"

The old man's head sank down between his shoulders as he started scarfing down the calabaza flan his daughter had set in front of him.

"Can't talk to anybody in this house. All everybody does is criticize me," he let out after a short pause.

Zé smiled and said nothing. She started washing the dishes her father had used. She gazed out the window now and then to watch some kids playing stickball in the middle of the street. She put the plate, glass, and utensils up to drain, dried her hands on the kitchen towel, and went over to one of the windows that looked out on the street.

"Watch out for cars, don't get yourselves run over!" she shouted. "And be careful not to break any of the wind- shields on the parked cars!"

Sitting down in one of the wicker-backed rocking chairs by the window, she closed her eyes, threw her head back, and let the breeze blowing in through the window grate cool her face.

She could see Petros, at eight or nine years old, learning to play piano with Tía Adela. She remembered her mother coming through the door of their house in Matanzas with Osiris, fresh out of prison. The warm reception by her tía, always so loving.

She also conjured up the letters from one of her best girlfriends, the only one who bothered answering her letters, where she told Zé that she'd fallen in love with a man older than her, and then another man, also older, and that she was leaving for Paris, and that she'd write her from there. And so she did, as promised. Her letters came by the oddest routes, always half-open or opened and clumsily resealed. She invariably asked about Petros, her mother, her aunt, Osiris. Until the political police paid a visit to ask her what sort of relations she had with Yocandra, given that Yocan- dra couldn't maintain relations with people like her. Yocan- dra was the wife of a diplomat, while Zé was the daughter of a lesbian living in the home of a prostitute, a criminal, also lesbian, who'd been in prison . . . Zé stopped him cold, assuring him that her only relationship with Yocandra was that they had gone to the same school in Havana, that she was living in Matanzas now and Yocandra in Paris, and that she hadn't gotten any letters from her in a long time, nor was she ever planning to answer a single letter of hers in the future. In this way she hindered or halted whatever trouble she knew she might cause her friend.

It was a long time before either of them wrote again. Yocandra was now an exile, still in Paris. But nowadays letters could come and go with travelers or tourists, and very few people cared about the old incidents that had branded her family so unjustly.

In one of these latter-day letters, Yocandra asked her, "How did you all manage, in the terrible situation you were in, to make Petros the artist that he's become?" Zé asked herself this every day. How? And she had an answer: love overcame all, the love of four women who put every effort into educating their "tiny genius," as she jokingly called her son.

Adela taught him to master musical instruments, her mother and Osiris told him about his Cuban and Greek origins, and she studied and worked to feed him, to be with him every night and read children's books to him, and to check on his progress at school.

None of this was sufficient, though. Petros became a real talent, but it was only after his grandfather talked to the higher-ups, pulled a few strings, and got the loan of a theater where his grandson could put on a concert that he became the recognized musical artist he was today— and even then, only because he had a very lucky break: on the first night of the concert, he captivated a French music promoter with his tremendous outpouring of charisma and his genius in combining the traditional music of two countries, Cuba and Greece. That was how the young man gained such prestige as a musician in so short a time. So in the end, it was thanks to his grandfather and to the French impresario, who started managing his career from overseas, and who moreover paid huge sums to the government every time the kid played abroad.

All the talent in the world would have done nothing for Petros if he hadn't had this grandfather, who still had a bit of power in high places, and if the impresario hadn't happened to be there that night at the first concert he'd done in his life. She knew this, and of course so did Petros.

She couldn't help but be aware that a whole skein of macabre strands was being woven between the impresario and Gerardo's former colleagues as time went on. One day, one of those strands might snap. Nor was she unaware that a rope always breaks at its weakest strand. The weakest strand was Petros. And she never neglected to warn him about the possibility that one day he might find himself at the peak of his art's popularity, and the next day in the depths of a swamp.

HER SON WAS ten when Zé shouldered the task of explaining to him that his father was a foreigner, a man born not in Cuba but in Greece, and that she'd never seen him since that last time, the time he left her pregnant. Being the son of a foreigner in this country meant bearing a heavy political burden on his shoulders. His father was a foreigner. And to top it off, a Greek merchant marine sailor. They had fallen in love very young and she had wanted to have their child: him.

While she spoke to him in her sweet voice, Petros stared fixedly at her. At last he sighed and said, "I know where Greece is, Mamá, I've found it on the world map at school. It won't be hard to go visit Papá."

Then she had to go on explaining, which got harder and harder. The trouble was that they couldn't travel to Greece or anywhere else in the world because, as Cubans, they weren't allow to leave the country freely. Also, Petros shouldn't tell anybody what she had just told him. Not ever.

"Why not, Mamá?"

"Because it's wrong for a woman to have children with a foreigner."

"Then why is Katiuska's father a foreigner and a Soviet technician and he talks Russian?" Petros was referring to a little classmate whose father was a military trainer from Moscow who had married a Cuban woman.

"It's complicated, Petros." She was about to tell him

that everything in this whole damn country is complicated, but she thought better of it. "Katiuska's father isn't a regular foreigner, he's, um, he's a . . . He's a Soviet brother, and so long as the Party authorizes it you can do whatever you want with our Soviet brothers."

"Why aren't Greeks our brothers, like Soviets?"

"Well, um," she wavered. "Because Greeks aren't Soviets, and that's that. And stop bugging me with stupid questions."

"I'm not stupid, I'm not! I know Greeks aren't Soviets! And I also know that Greeks aren't Yankees. So if they aren't our enemies and they aren't our friends, what are they?"

"Greeks. I already told you." Zé sighed, rolling her eyes. "Greek sailors."

"Why did you give me such a problem for a father?"

"I fell in love, it was love at first sight. I wasn't really thinking. The follies of youth. That's why I'm always asking you to think things through twice, even three times, so you don't make mistakes that can't be undone."

"Was it a mistake to have me with a Greek father?"

Zé knelt down in front of him. "No, Petros, no! It wasn't. My mistake was not ever wanting to tell him about . . . Never mind, we'll continue this conversation some other day."

"He doesn't know I exist? Is that it?"

"Petros, son, I couldn't, I mean . . . No. He doesn't know." Her eyes teared up.

"What's my papá's name?"

"Orestes."

"How old is he now?"

"Same age as me. He must be a grown man now. A man of the sea. We were a couple of kids when we met. We fell in love the first time we saw each other, though we knew we had to keep our relationship a secret. Tía Osiris helped us do that, and later on Abuela, and Tía Adela, too. But Abuelo Gerardo got very angry, and—"

"Is that why he never wants to see us?" The boy picked up a pen and started doodling in a notebook.

"Yes, that's why, but someday he'll change. Abuelo will change. You'll see."

The child looked up.

"Mamá, can I go out and play now?"

"You have your guitar lesson."

"And after that?"

"We're going to do something very nice for both of us. Today you can finish your class early and go play."

"Really?"

"Yes, if you'll promise me one thing. You can't tell anybody outside of the family about what we were just discussing. When you want to talk and find out more about your father, you and I can do that, just the two of us. Or you can talk with Abuela, with Osiris, and with Adela, they know everything. Osiris knew your father, and your father's father, your paternal grandfather. But you can only talk with us—okay?"

"Yes, Mamá." He smiled, kissed her cheek, and ran off to find his guitar.

After that day, Zé devoted herself to studying Greek culture in greater depth. She taught herself Greek. She went to Havana to watch Greek films, or films about Greece, at the art movie houses. Since she couldn't tell her son much about his father, given that she didn't know all that much about him herself, she decided to teach him about his paternal origins and use culture to make up for the tenderness of an absent father.

SHE WAS TWENTY-SEVEN when Ignacio appeared in her life. Up until then she had gone out informally with a few men, but never before with one who proposed to marry her and who also added that he'd raise the boy as his own. Her son would soon turn eleven, so he was already almost done with being raised, but there was no denying that Ignacio had been sensitive in proposing to her in this way.

They had met at one of the intensive courses she attended in Havana. He was also from Matanzas, and they were both staying at the hotel where the organizers had housed people from their province. Luckily for them, it was the Deauville, an oceanfront hotel where only foreign technical experts from the Soviet Union were usually allowed to stay, though with the havoc caused by perestroika the Soviets were showing up less and less often.

They met at the hotel restaurant. She was eating by herself, as was he, at an adjoining table. So he asked the waitress for permission to move to his colleague's table.

"May I?" he then asked her, his plate in one hand and glass in the other.

Zé agreed, though grudgingly. She preferred to eat alone and avoid the company of people with whom she knew she would share only the study of literature or philosophy and little or nothing else.

"I'm Ignacio," he introduced himself, slightly embarrassed.

"I know. I saw your name on the list of participants, and

at the session today the professor mentioned your work and praised it. I'm Zé." She reached over to shake his hand.

He opened his mouth as if to say something but she interrupted him. "Yes, I know that, too; it's an unusual name. That's what everybody tells me."

"Your name? Unusual? No, not at all. I was just going to ask if you liked the hotel."

"We got lucky. It's a hotel for the elite. I think they put us up here by mistake."

Without answering, he sought out her gaze. They both laughed.

"They put us up in this hotel because every other hotel was taken by Party members. Don't forget, the Party congress is in session."

"I guess I skipped that session."

They laughed.

"Not much of a session," he pointed out, and they laughed harder.

That night Ignacio invited her for a stroll along the Malecón after dinner, and from then on they were never apart. They got married six months later. Ignacio was divorced, no kids, thirty-one. Handsome, intense green eyes, smooth skin, black hair, a body sculpted by daily exercise, and very cultured.

He didn't find it odd that she was unmarried and had a child. Nor did he ask too many questions about it.

And so their story began: all of a sudden.

After they married, he preferred to have her move into

the place where he had been living alone, which looked out onto the beautiful bay of Matanzas. He was a calm, quiet man who loved and cared for Petros. The boy, however, preferred staying at Tía Adela's house, along with Abuela Isabel and Osiris. Petros and Ignacio got along well, but Ignacio knew that the boy would never see him as his father, while for his part he had never been all that interested in children. Still, he made an effort with Petros, trying to care for him like the father who had never been by the boy's side.

Zé loved Ignacio and he loved her. But they had each been in love before, too intensely, with two people now beyond their reach. Ignacio's ex-wife had left him to go to the United States with her parents. Ignacio had never wanted to leave the country, and they decided on a divorce, by mutual agreement, before she left.

The night they decided to go to bed together, Zé admitted to him, "I've never felt what I felt with Orestes again. With anyone. We fell in love so fast. It was my first love."

"What are you expecting from me, then?"

"I'm hoping for *el gran amor*. Again. For *el big love* to catch me, take me in its arms, and make me fly. I want you to make me fly!"

"I'll make you fly. I'll try. I also want to be what you call *el big love*."

"Until death does us part," she said, laughing.

"Nothing can part us," Ignacio whispered, looking straight into her eyes.

He took her by the hand and led her a few steps to the bed. He slipped the formfitting dress from Zé's body, and she began to undress him. Never taking their eyes off each other. They kissed, a long kiss.

Their kiss went on for years, with pauses on both sides, but their ardor never lessened; what did begin to melt away was the tenderness.

There was nothing extraordinary about the end of tenderness on Ignacio's part. She noticed his growing distance, not with bitterness, but suffering it in silence.

As Zé became more of a woman and found more success in her career, Ignacio grew more resentful, never achieving the same level as Zé. A moderate success, only as much as could be allowed within a totalitarian society where no person can stand out more than expected, and never more than the bosses.

"It's incredible how much luck you have, like the angels are protecting you. I've been begging for years to get transferred to the University of Havana and fighting for the position, and here they offer it to you without your even asking for it."

"It isn't luck, Ignacio. I submitted a librarianship plan for improved access to reading, is all."

"You aren't even a Party member, and they pave the way for you like that."

"Nobody paves the way for me, I find my own way, through my own work."

"Isn't your father behind all this?"

"All my father wants is to see me as far away from him as possible. Even better, dead. He's said as much, on several occasions: he'd rather have a daughter who's dead than a 'Greek whore.'"

"That's all in the past. You're married to me now. I'm a model for him." They both smiled.

"I never understood why you worked so hard to join the Party when you never believed in it."

Ignacio raised a finger to his lips. "Hush, the walls have ears. Party membership opens doors; you know that."

"As you just said, I'm not a member, and still more doors get opened for me than for you. Ignacio, sometimes intelligence is all it takes."

"Are you trying to say that I'm not as intelligent as you?" For the first time she noticed the flare of resentment in his eyes.

"I'm trying to say that I've had more time than you to work on my projects. Don't you see how much time you waste on those boring meetings where they always say the same thing about remaining loyal to the Great Leader?" Zé raised her hand to her chin and stroked an imaginary long, patriarchal beard.

"True. And maybe I'm bringing you luck, don't you think? I bring you luck that you can't bring me."

Zé was stunned, but she wanted to think he was joking. She should have seen it coming, the blow that would hit her years later, at the very moment when Ignacio let loose with such idiocy. But she preferred to think that it was a fit of jealousy, an ungentlemanly and rather jealous or envious remark, and she let it pass.

"Remember that movie we watched at Tía Adela's house, on the Sunday show—*Love Story*? Remember the part about—"

"*Love means never having to say you're sorry*. Is that the quote you mean? Why do you always throw that quote at me, like a kind of reprimand?"

No, it wasn't a reprimand. It was just a reminder, a precautionary measure, so that neither of them would have to say they were sorry someday for some nonsense that might destroy their true love.

But while Zé was living for the love of her son and her husband, and her family, and her studies and work, Ignacio for his part was dying to be given a good position at the University of Havana, the same sort of position they'd just given his wife, and all he thought about was how to attain what she had already accomplished.

"Look, I've made up my mind, I'm not going to take the job. It's too complicated a teaching position, and besides, we'd have to move to Havana, and I love it here in Matanzas." She tried to wrap up the conversation on the subject, which had cropped up multiple times in various places and in different guises: in a curt argument at home, in a quiet conversation at a restaurant, during a stroll along the beach near Varadero.

"You can't do that. Don't you see how stupid it would be not to accept it?" Ignacio took her hand, feeling guilty.

"It's for the best, Ignacio. Nothing can separate us, least of all this." Her teary eyes turned gray as the sea. Out there before them, the light roar of the autumn waves dampened the sound of their voices.

"You'd sacrifice your career for me? Are you sure?" He took his wife's chin in his fingers with a certain pride, contemplating the beauty of her gaze. "My god, you have the most beautiful eyes in the world."

"I'd sacrifice everything for Petros and for you. My life is a triangle, the two of you and me. Petros at the top, you and me at the base. That's how I wanted to make it."

This triangle wasn't entirely to Ignacio's liking. He thought that, as the head of household, he should be at the top, the highest point, and not at the same level as her. He felt that Petros was far too young to indicate what guidelines to follow, much less be the tip of an arrow that might hit any bull's-eye.

"Pay a little more attention to me, Zé. You've already spent too much time on Petros. He's not a baby anymore. He'll find his own way."

And so he did. Petros found his own way, the way of music, becoming a virtuoso guitar player, pianist, percussionist; he also had a beautiful voice for singing the Cuban *son*, and he performed classic Greek songs that came from his soul as if he'd spent his whole life in his real father's country. None of this made Ignacio happy. The more time went by, the more jealous he grew of the shadow of an unknown man. The shadow of the absent father. And the more envious of his stepson's talent.

He still enjoyed Zé in bed as a woman, but after all these years he could think of her only as the woman who showed up in his life and stopped the process of his personal growth and success. So even though she devoted all her efforts, her energy, and the money she earned to boosting Ignacio's intellectual projects, he couldn't recognize what she had contributed to him, only what she had supposedly taken away, imagining her to be an immovable barrier. And what she had taken away was the time he had invested, according to him, in raising Petros.

A woman in love never sees things so clearly as when the man she loves starts making mistakes and leaving traces of those mistakes behind on the field of his indifference. The loved man, sure of being loved, indirectly falls into making those mistakes on purpose; he might even commit them without any sort of malice, though in a selfish way, with a fierce selfishness, and thoughtlessly, as if using them to shield his pride. A woman in love almost always has a kind of veil across her soul and only glances sidelong at the evidence, in terror, reluctantly. A woman in love becomes a fearful woman after it is already too late and the viper's fangs have sunk two holes deep into her pride.

Ignacio left her because he wanted to live alone and

get a better job in Havana that would allow him, of course, to earn more money, which according to his calculations could never happen so long as he lived with her.

He walked out, leaving the house to her but hoping to get it back as soon as he could. Which really upset his new lover, a foreign woman, a tourist. Yes, Ignacio had felt a predilection for tourists lately. He found them better, superior in every way, disparaging Cuban women first with oblique, hypocritical words and later more directly, something he constantly did in front of Zé, never holding his tongue.

"Cuban women are getting grosser all the time. All they want to do is get the hell out of Cuba. They've turned prostitution into their ticket to the 'great beyond.' Meanwhile, foreign women who come here as tourists are in awe of the country they're discovering. They surrender to the adventure of living among us, with all our pluses and minuses. Cuban women have lost elegance, respect. I don't know. They don't like their place, they don't have an ounce of self-respect. At least the women of Matanzas still have a little of that, because Havana women have lost all shame."

"How can you say stuff like that about Cuban women and Havana women? I'm from Havana, and I'm not shameless. Don't tell me the tourist women have rendered you brain dead. Or have you come down with speculator-boss syndrome? A joint venture or a foreign-owned business would bring in more cash than a Cuban job. Welcome to savage capitalism!"

Ignacio was buttoning up his newly ironed shirt. He left off doing that and grabbed her abruptly by the shoulders. He instantly realized the mistake he'd made and let go of her, but he pointed his finger accusingly and shouted, "Don't you speak to me in that tone! Never again! I'm not going to put up with you anymore! I've had it up to here with your prissy little lectures! You're the last one who should be lecturing me—you, number one in adoring foreigners in our country, number one in betraying even your own father, going to bed with one of them. And with a dirty Greek, no less. You, the fucking whore, the fucking Greek whore! A Greek sailor's whore!"

That was it. No more, she told him, tears in her eyes. Right then, at that moment, she saw their whole life together glide past as if on screen, like in a third-rate movie. That same afternoon she ended the relationship in which she had invested the most important part of her life and finished her marriage, which had tied her to that man until the end of their days.

Of course, Ignacio didn't live alone for long. One month and ten days later, after an odyssey around Havana, he installed a female tourist in the apartment that one of his best friends had loaned him. A genuine whore, picked up at a hotel for single Latin American women ravenous for whatever was put before them, male or female. A specimen halfway between hippie and vintage revolutionary, with a touch of phony Frida Kahlo thrown in for good measure.

Eighteen years younger than him. One of those climbers; a homewrecker. The sort that hangs around gullible Cuban men in hopes of getting bankrolled by a tropical dick. And of getting him to bend over backward, work like the devil for her for the rest of his life, by becoming the chick of his dreams and ambitions. Only to toss him aside in the end, like a worn-out rag doll.

Zé felt desolate, devasted, for months. Ignacio's attitude of absolute contempt and detachment stirred up the pain and agony of a number of half-healed wounds: her abandonment by Orestes, his disappearance, her abandonment by her father, her being accused by the mob of betraying the country, followed by the taunts and derision aimed at her and her mother.

You always can learn from pain, that was something she had found out when she was very young; from solitude, too, even more so. Therefore she accepted her (somewhat) chosen solitude with humility. She swore that, from that moment on, there would be no other man in her life than her son. Petros, the fruit of her youthful passion. Petros was her finest work, the product of her first love.

PART II

Arsen,
or
Πάθος

THE FLIGHT FROM Havana to Paris took longer than it should have. The Cubana plane had defects, and they made us return three times to where we had taken off, José Martí International Airport.

I was scared to death, always thinking they were bringing the plane back on purpose, to remove me from the flight and leave me grounded, forbidden to travel. Petros held my hand again each time to reassure me, giving it a light squeeze. From our seats in the first row of economy class we could see, up until the plane finally took off for good and the flight attendants yanked closed the curtain that separated us from the Cuban officials in first class, how they too kept turning back to monitor us.

At last we arrived in Paris. What a shock to see two of the highest-ranking officials—including Captain Fandiñas, the very same who had interviewed me to determine whether I should be allowed to travel to Greece, my father's oh-so-revolutionary friend—jump the line and make a straight dash to the French authorities, requesting political asylum at the top of their lungs.

Petros and I were trembling, I could feel it in the way he pressed my arm, but we kept our lips shut tight. The only official who remained on our side, who looked just as shocked as we were, immediately came over and whispered to us, "Would you two do that?"

We nervously shook our heads no.

"I wouldn't stay here either for anything in the world. I have my wife and children back there. But so do those guys who just ran away, and they didn't care. But I do. I wouldn't. I'm sorry, my name is Luis. Luis Muñoz."

Neither Petros nor I knew him. We shook his hand. He did know who we were, naturally. He was plainly a new functionary and very glum at the moment, after what had just happened.

"They'll investigate us here in France," he complained. "And I'm not sure which side will do it, the French or the Cuban police."

Indeed, as we exited the airport on our way to another airport, where we were to catch the plane to Greece the next morning, we were intercepted by two men in plain clothes who said they worked for the Cuban embassy in Paris.

"Where are you going?" they asked, after identifying themselves and revealing to us, as if by accident, that they each wore a holster bearing a bulky pistol.

"We were going to go to one of those Ibis hotels near the other airport to spend the night there. Tomorrow we'll be flying to Athens. We're musicians. Well, not me—he's the musician," Luis said, pointing to Petros, "I'm an official in the Ministry of Culture, and she . . ." He hesitated, with a complicit glance in my direction. "She writes essays on Greek topics. On Greek music."

The man took a drag on an e-cigarette.

"We know all about the three of you and the others who got away. My question is: where do you think they're going?" He made his question sound like a threat.

The guy who was with us didn't answer him, just gave an ironic smile.

"Given what's happened, you'll have to come with us to the embassy," the apparent boss of the operation went on.

"But we have to leave for Athens tomorrow," Luis protested.

"We'll see about that. Tonight, you're sleeping at the embassy. Consider yourselves detained."

Petros was about to protest, but I quietly signaled him to stop.

They positioned themselves on either side of Petros and me, with the functionary in the middle, and discreetly pushed us toward the airport parking garage.

We were forced into a Peugeot. The one who hadn't said a word until then asked for the keys, and the other tossed them over the car to him. The second one said, "I'll drive, you sit in the back with the mother and son. I'll control this one."

And that was that. We sat obediently as we left the garage. It was raining buckets in Paris. I was so filled with worry that I scarcely looked at the city I had been so excited to see when we arrived. Besides, the heavy downpour was like a curtain, separating us on all sides from the normal goings-on of Parisians.

We pulled into the garage of a hideous building surrounded by walls and fencing. There they took us upstairs
to some even uglier cheaply furnished offices. The interrogation went on for the rest of the day and all night.

After several calls to Havana, the most senior officials
in the Cuban Foreign Ministry—or rather, in the Foreign
Ministry and the Ministry of Culture, who in turn con-
sulted with their respective military bosses in the Ministry
of the Interior—they decided that Luis Muñoz, the functionary, would stay with us for the rest of the trip. Because
they had never questioned whether Petros and I should be
able to travel. On the contrary, what they were wondering
was whether the functionary was sufficiently trustworthy
or whether he'd defect as the others had, but only after
stealing the money he was to be paid in Greece for Petros's
show. The only one who really mattered was Petros, since
they'd be taking a sizeable cut from his concerts' earnings.

Then me, only because I was his mother; they didn't
think of me at all as a prominent writer. To understand
the situation, after all, they had talked with several of my
father's friends, and with my father himself. That was where
we discovered that, despite his age, Papá was still collabo-
rating with the secret police, for the sole purpose of making our lives, and perhaps my mother's life, easier. That's
what I could gather from eavesdropping on the conversa-
tions that were going on, with Petros and me as witnesses.

We barely slept two hours, sprawled across three of the

uncomfortable sofas in the embassy. Early the next morning, the same State Security officials drove us back in the same car to the airport, where a few hours later we caught the plane to Athens.

It had stopped raining in Paris. On the way to the airport I enjoyed the view of a magnificent city awash in sunlight, where I would have loved to live. Even to have been born.

"You like Paris, comrade?" the police asked me, in an old spoilsport tone from the Cold War, looking at me less aggressively now in the rearview mirror.

"I like what I'm seeing," I answered briefly.

"And you, Petros?"

Petros didn't hesitate: "I like Havana better." His answer was more intelligent than mine, after all.

Our interrogator didn't believe a word of it.

WHEN HE PICKED up our bags after landing at the Athens airport, Petros finally relaxed and smiled. Luis Muñoz, the functionary, was in a rush to get out of the terminal.

"We have to hurry, the director of the music publisher that booked Petros for the Athens concert is waiting for us, and it looks like they've added a few more concerts. He told me he was going to come himself, which is a very nice gesture for someone in his position." Muñoz also seemed less tense. "Now let's do what we do best: make music. I should explain that I'm a musicologist, that's what I studied in college, but I had to become a bureaucrat because, well, what choice did I have? You two know how that mambo goes."

"You don't have to explain anything to us, Luis, please." Petros patted the careworn man on the back.

"Thank you, thank you, thank you," he repeated three times in genuine gratitude, relieved.

The sliding doors opened. A crowd of people waited outside, some carrying signs and placards with passengers' names. A tall man with graying hair, about fifty-something years old, hurried to greet us; he was dressed in a white shirt and light blue jeans. He introduced himself. "I am Arsen Tziolis, owner of Aires, the music publisher." As he spoke, he looked only at me, holding my hand for a long time.

At last he pulled himself together, let go of my hand, and shook Petros's and Luis's. "Allow me to carry your suitcase," he told me, still seeking my gaze.

"There's no need, it doesn't weigh anything," I replied in some embarrassment.

"Well, but, it's my custom to be carrying the ladies' luggage."

He was perfectly fluent in Spanish, which he had learned while studying in Spain, as well as French, having gone to college in France, as he explained to us. We had a very pleasant conversation in the car.

He drove us to the hotel where we had made reservations, in the Monastiraki neighborhood, and showed us some of the city on the way: the Parliament building, a few neighborhoods. He began to complain about politicians and how they were plunging the country into total catastrophe. Good thing he didn't ask about Cuba and its politicians, not to mention the officials who were supposed to have come with us but had requested asylum in France.

He did say, however: "I found out a little late about what happened in Paris, but I must admit I'm happy not to have to put up with the representative who was supposed to come with you, since we already had arguments with him over the phone and couldn't really come to an understanding." He paused. "And you, Petros? Always so quiet?"

Petros shook his head no, but he was smiling.

"You're a great artist, kid." Arsen had gotten Petros to sit next to him. "I hope you find what you're looking for in Greece, though you are the one with talent. Talent and a mixed heritage. There is much that you could offer Greece."

"Yes, thanks to my mother's courage," Petros announced, and I sensed that he had concentrated the whole meaning of his life and mine into this phrase. "I'm half Greek."

"No doubt about it, kid, no doubt. I know about your origins, half Greek. Thank you, Señora Zé, thank you for having such a hardworking son." He sought out my eyes in the rearview mirror. I nodded in agreement, smiling, and he went on. "What would you all wish to do tonight?"

"For me, frankly, begging everyone's pardon, but I'd rather go to sleep, I'm so tired," Muñoz said. "But if the rest of you want to go out, please go ahead without me."

Arsen paid little attention to the bureaucrat's excuse.

"I was thinking of taking you all to eat at a place where you'll have a view of the Parthenon illuminated at night. It is a gorgeous sight. Only if you wish, of course. We can take advantage of the time to discuss the concerts we've scheduled. Although I would understand if you're exhausted. Better if we go tomorrow, and—"

Petros interrupted him. "I'd rather go out tonight. What about you, Mamá? I imagine you would, too."

I agreed, my eyes dodging Arsen's, which he only took off mine in the mirror to attend to the traffic.

"I am inviting you to dinner then. Tomorrow we shall meet with you, Señor Muñoz."

"You can call me Luis. Thank you very much," the bureaucrat agreed.

"And all of you can call me Arsen. Or whatever you find easier—Arsenio, Arseni."

"Arsen is beautiful," I said, shifting my gaze to look out the window, which I opened to let the air cool my face.

"Zé is also a very attractive name," he said, continuing to burn his gaze into me.

After we got to the hotel, while we were waiting for them to get our rooms ready, Arsen wanted us to go up to the top floor for a pleasant surprise. From the broad roof-top terrace, which sported a swimming pool and a café bar, we had a beautiful view of the Parthenon towering into a clear blue sky. My eyes filled with tears. Petros put his arm around my shoulders and held me tight.

Luis Muñoz pulled his little camera out of a bag that he never put down. "Ay, if only my wife and my kids could see this!" he repeated, deeply moved.

Arsen called over the waitress and ordered an afternoon snack for everyone. Delicious traditional Greek appetizers and iced tea. After a while he said he had to leave us and get back to his office, where his work awaited. He'd be back to pick us up at eight on the dot that evening.

THERE'S SOMETHING VERY singular about Havana nights: the stars that hover above ruined buildings seem to lift them up bodily. But the ruins of Havana embitter the people who are forced to live in them. Totally unlike Greek ruins, which are also gently rocked by the stellar glow that penetrates their stones, making the timeworn alabaster glimmer as if about to boil, rocking the ruins and cradling us.

Arsen arrived right on schedule in his car to pick up Petros and me. He preferred to park the car in the hotel garage and for us all to walk to the restaurant. As we did.

Night fell and the blanket of stars spread over us before we noticed. Arsen showed us the shortest way, the least crowded way, to get to the Parthenon. It was a dark road that wound around several important monuments, including the cavern where Socrates supposedly drank the fatal hemlock.

Petros and Arsen started discussing the concerts. The first in Athens; two more in Crete; and they'd close with one more in Athens, the last.

"Though I don't think you will actually close with that concert, because if everything goes as well as I expect, you'll be invited many more times," Arsen said. "Tickets are sold out; the next thing is to wait and see how the concert critics react."

He treated Petros like a friend, as if he'd known him his whole life, and yet he addressed him with respect and admiration, especially because of his music, which fascinated him, signifying that he was more deeply moved by art than by business—though of course, making a profit was also important.

On the walk over, which took about half an hour, he asked me several questions, anxious to learn more than he probably knew already; in other words, he probed into my life.

"Why do you love this country so much? What led up to this?"

"It's a long story. Anyway, I specialize in Greece. I mean, I've studied it in depth."

"That much I've heard. But were you so totally, totally into Greek that you even gave your son a Greek name?"

"Yes, I was *totally totally* into Greece," I replied without hesitation.

"My father is Greek," Petros responded, as if to give me a hand.

"Ah, that is news! Wonderful! Does he live in Cuba? Why didn't he come with you?"

"No, he doesn't live in Cuba. I don't know him." Petros shrugged, feeling uncomfortable.

"I, well, me, I barely know him either, I mean, I'd hardly recognize him today," I noted, equally uncomfortable. "We were just teenagers, we had a fling, a youthful adventure. Our son was born of that. He left Cuba never knowing I was pregnant. Orestes was the son of the captain of a Greek ship, merchant marine. And he was a cabin boy."

"I'm sorry." Now he was the one feeling uncomfortable with the information I'd given him so directly. "Might there not be some way of finding him here, I mean, of tracing him?"

"We'd love to, but it'd be almost impossible. All I have is his name. But it wouldn't be advisable for us to do it. Not sure if you understand my meaning."

"Mamá, things aren't like that in Cuba anymore. Making money is the only thing those people care about now. If we went looking for my father, it wouldn't mean anything to them."

"But it would to your grandfather, and you know it." I side-eyed Petros.

"There's no reason Abuelo has to find out. And Abuela Isabel and Tía Osiris would be thrilled for their part, and it would also make Tía Adela happy if we found Papá."

"The main ones who need to be happy are you two, no?" Arsen broke in.

"Forgive us, Arsen. We shouldn't be arguing like this in front of you." Was I getting too friendly with him?

"Oh, please, of course you may talk about anything you wish in front of me. And also, I'm fine if you treat me like a friend—if that is all right with the two of you." He threw an arm across Petros's shoulders and took me by the elbow. He was walking in the middle. We looked like a family out for a stroll.

"What is the full name of Petros's father?" Arsen asked.

"I could try to look into the matter without either of you becoming involved."

"Orestes Thalassinos. It was hard just finding out what his last name was. I couldn't remember it. Thanks, Osiris . . ."

"We shall see, we shall see. Nothing is impossible. We will put in some inquiries," Arsen murmured.

"For my own part, I'd like my son and his father to meet each other," I muttered too. "It isn't even a desire. More than that, it's a dream."

The restaurant was near a movie theater. It faced the Parthenon, with a beautiful rooftop terrace. That's where we sat. I had never imagined that someday I'd be able to contemplate such a monument in all its majesty, skillfully illuminated, with the mantle of stars lending it outsized magnificence.

Our new friend ordered dinner for us. He was excited to introduce us to a lot of traditional Greek dishes and desserts, intent on getting us to sample and taste the essence of his country's cuisine. A pair of candles lit the table, and Arsen's face, deep down, looked profoundly sad to me. Brown eyes, shy smile, but sure in his speech, large hands. I thought I might fall in love with this man, but I immediately swept the notion from my mind.

"I'm going to put my cards down on the table. I know what is happening in Cuba. I know a few Cuban exiles. You don't have to pretend with me. I'm ready to help. In other words, you may be frank with me—no worries."

"We haven't had the worst of it, though my mother has a very particular story. Other people have gone over Niagara on a bicycle—meaning, they've had worse things happen to them. And that's all I have to say." That's how Petros always responded; that's how I had raised him, training him to always protect himself when confronting any sort of provocation. "So is everything all wrapped up for the concert?"

"Everything is set, you don't have to worry about absolutely anything." Arsen turned to smile at me, sweetly, tenderly. "It is admirable: women who raise their children on their own prepare them to live in the most essential way, because it's all about living, essentially about living."

All three of us laughed, aware of what he was referring to. Standing tall in the distance, the Parthenon reigned in all its majesty, a mystery of the ages. The night was full of a slight, surprising scent of burnt jasmine. The aroma reminded me of a Havana night in the garden of an old mansion I used to visit in the Cerro neighborhood.

WHILE PETROS WAS out rehearsing with Greek and Latin American musicians, I would go for walks on my own, losing myself among the many historic sites that abound in Athens. I'd ramble among monuments, some of them reduced to sumptuous rubble, or visit museums, spending hours engrossed in one or another of the sculptures and historical objects I had so often dreamed of, having seen and studied them so often in books. I was brimming with joy, a strange joy. This was my first trip abroad, and I was finding the world a nice place to be, not at all as vicious as we'd been told.

I might be capable of living there, in Athens. I could rent a tiny room somewhere and go on being as happy as I felt right now. But no, forget it; I wasn't ready to leave my country, but most of all I couldn't stop thinking about my folks. I had to return, had to go back with my son, who had promised to return me to them, like I was one more musical instrument on the tour. That was the pact, the deal Petros had cut to get them to authorize my trip. I could travel, sure, but his fate as an artist depended in turn on my going back. His career was hanging by a thread. That's what they had led him to believe.

Sometimes Arsen joined me on these rambles. We'd mainly talk about Cuba, about politics, about how everything was going downhill in Greece too, and suddenly we were somehow starting to talk about our own lives. I jumped into my whole story. I ended up admitting to him, "I've never felt myself truly loved. I've always been the one doing the loving."

"Well, if you know anything about world literature, which I know you do," he said, "that story is as old as humanity. The dilemma of love, the riddle of who is truly happy—the one who loves, or the one who is loved. I have always preferred loving. I had one irreplaceable love—my wife, the mother of my children—and that is how it will always be. Yes, dear Zé, there are good men. Sentimental, faithful in love, loyal to their love. Though they call us fools. As you can tell, I am one of those few."

I understood what he was trying to tell me. It was a warning. Watch out, there won't be anything between us, there can't be. I lowered my eyes, walking with my eyes glued to the cobblestones. All the great Greek heroes, my heroes, had trodden these same stones. These same stones were the ones that Orestes had walked on, and perhaps still did.

He guessed what I was thinking.

"I was investigating the name you gave me. I found someone with the same name as your son's father. He lives in Chania, near the harbor, on Crete. When we're there for Petros's concert, we can go visit him. If you wish. I have already called and spoken to him, and yes, he was in Havana with his father when he was a teenager. And, yes, he remembers a fling with a girl very much like the one who stands here before me."

My heart started beating fast. My palms grew sweaty. For a moment I couldn't speak. At last I replied.

"I was thinking of him. What you're saying has shocked me. I'll have to tell Petros and get his opinion. I don't know what to do . . ."

"I have already told him. I apologize if I got ahead of myself. He is in agreement with going to visit him. I also gave the gentleman in question a brief explanation of what it was about, and of course he was astonished, dumbstruck. He raised no objection to seeing his son—or his first girlfriend."

I couldn't contain my emotions. I threw myself into Arsen's arms. Big, strong, safe arms. I wept against his chest, curled against him. Feeling shame, I pushed away.

We were skirting around the ancient agora, and the sun was hotter than ever.

When I got back to the hotel, Petros and I looked at each other and immediately understood, without saying a word, that we were of the same mind. We'd go visit Orestes Thalassinos, his father, in Chania, where he presumably lived.

Luis Muñoz, the Cuban official, got back late. He always got back late, because after his meetings he'd go shopping to see what he could get for his family with the tiny allowance they'd allotted us. Looking worn out, he surveyed us with a sad smile.

"What a beautiful country! What stores they have!" he exclaimed.

Yes, both Petros and I had the same thought. Instead of visiting the ruins of ancient Greece, what remained of it and its immense culture, Muñoz never tired of shopping in the stores on Ermou, the busiest pedestrian mall in the Plaka neighborhood, with its many shops. He spent all his time buying trinkets to bring home as gifts for his family.

Petros's concert in Athens was a resounding success with both the audience and the press. There wasn't room for one more soul inside the Megaro Mousikis concert hall; tickets had sold out right away and were even being resold at jacked-up prices. Arsen, next to me, couldn't believe the audience enthusiasm.

"I suspected it would be a hit, but I didn't expect anything so legendary as this," he said, ecstatic.

Petros had performed better than ever. For my own part, I had been certain it would turn out exactly the way it did. I had watched his musician self outgrow everything else about him, outgrow even his reasonable teenage rebelliousness. Music was everything to Petros, and the combination of Greek and Cuban music added up to the true meaning of his origins and his talent. Just seeing him so happy, high-fiving the young fans in the front row, moving around on stage like he was born to be there, overwhelmed me with emotion because it proved that having him, defending my right to give birth to my son, meant that now he could shine here with all his gifts, multitalented and radiant, being what he unquestionably was: an artist.

The next night we flew to Crete, where Petros was to give several concerts in beachfront hotels as well as in a small venue in Chania.

Our bureaucrat, Muñoz, decided to stay behind in Athens, arguing that he had to work out pending deals regarding other Cuban musicians. On hearing this, we breathed easier. His presence annoyed us simply because he acted like a bureaucrat.

Sitting next to me on the plane, Arsen pointed out the window and whispered into my ear, "Look, Zé, a full moon. That is a good omen."

I always follow the moon devotedly, as well as Venus, the star that chases the moon. I know they will invariably bring something good into my life.

AFTER THE PERFORMANCES in Knossos and Heraklion we decided to go to Chania, where Petros's father lived. We checked into a hotel by the beach in the neighboring village of Platanias, where my son would also be doing a show in a few days. Arsen accompanied us everywhere— attentive, wonderfully generous. I was amazed by each of these islands. Seeing them, I realized that the whole obsession we have about the island where I was born, off in the Caribbean, is nothing but another nationalistic contrivance aimed at brainwashing people. Each of these islands has its own unique beauty, which consists of how close the sea is, how blue the sky, and the sensation that every night the stars descend to celebrate the vitality of existence.

We arrived in Platanias on a Saturday. Arsen drove us there in a rental car. We settled into our rooms and went out early the next morning, planning to visit Orestes. I had already talked to him over the phone. He had warned me, thoughtfully, that he barely remembered me. He asked how I could be certain my son was his. I told him I hadn't had relations with any other man, either before or after I was with him, until Petros was born. Over the phone he sounded old but not gloomy; cheerful, rather. He had a wife and five children. Meeting his oldest son wouldn't create the slightest problem for him, for the same reason: he had grown old. Besides, from what he had heard, his son was famous and could earn a living without his father's help. He was curious to meet him, that's all. As for me, he said nothing to make me proud of having given him my virginity. He barely remembered our romance. I hadn't been important in his life, a fact I couldn't help but feel sad about. Because by contrast, he had been very important in mine. Not only was he the father of my only son, it was due to him that my whole family had broken apart. Because of him my family split up, and we spent years bouncing from one quarrel to the next. But it wasn't all his fault. "It's fate," I told myself. "Fate does what it will." And I remained engrossed in the immensity of the sea, walled off by olive trees. The most beautiful olive trees I've ever seen.

Tourists were beginning to crowd into Chania. Just setting foot in the village filled me with anxiety. I asked Petros and Arsen if we could stop a minute. We were right in front of a church. The sun was strong enough to break rocks. I was starting to feel ill. My body was bathed in cold sweat, and I had gone pale. Arsen suggested going into the church and sitting in the pews there for a while, so we did. Some women were restoring an ancient fresco inside. There was scaffolding everywhere. I imagined they must be restoring the rest of the sanctuary. People kept coming in anyway and kissing a painting of an icon. I went over and kissed it too. Petros copied me. Arsen deliberately lagged behind. I felt in better spirits, so we decided to continue walking to Orestes's house.

We walked around the harbor. The deep blue of the sea

reminded me of the afternoon I had spent by the bay of Havana, when I was a teenager and had to tell my parents I was pregnant. We turned into the narrow streets of the old town. Arsen pulled a slip of paper from his trouser pocket and unfolded it to check the address.

The building was next door to a "House of Love," a motel that looked exactly like one of the hourly-rate hotels used by lovers in Havana. We went up a flight and knocked on an aged door, painted blue. The gray-haired man who opened the door looked a lot like the father of Orestes. But it was Orestes himself, grown old, tanned by the sun and the sea, like any good, self-respecting sailor.

"Good afternoon, welcome," he said, and he studied first me from head to foot, then Petros.

The conversation continued in Spanish. Arsen explained how everything had come about and how he had found him, through a police inquiry.

"You already explained that to me over the phone, dear friend. I'm grateful."

Petros went up and gave his father a hug. He responded with emotion. We all three hugged. A woman peeked out from the adjoining room.

"Come, Marcia, come. She's my wife, the mother of my children—my other children," he added.

The woman, serious and quiet, shook our hands. She asked if we would like some water, coffee, fruit juice. We gladly accepted some lemonade. She disappeared, returning after a bit carrying a pitcher of cold lemonade and glasses on a tray.

"We were really hoping we could find you, Orestes, and let you know that you had a child in Cuba. Petros is a musician. He's come here to do a concert series. I've come along, as his mother."

Petros nodded his agreement with my words. "You're all invited to my concert in Chania. Please do come, if you'd like," Petros added with emotion.

"Thank you. We'll make an exception and go, only because it's you. We hardly ever leave the house. Just to visit our children, some of them married. They live in Knossos. Others work in Athens. That's why I don't think you'll get to meet them, they're always busy."

"On another occasion, Father, no worries," Petros replied very respectfully.

Here I was, looking at the man I had thought about my entire life, the man I'd dreamed about throughout my existence, and he was nothing like the idea I had formed of him.

"Orestes, do you remember anything about Havana?" I asked innocently.

"Yes, of course. I remember you, mainly you, and I vaguely recall the city," he lied, laughing. "After that I traveled a lot."

Then silence. A long, pin-drop silence.

"And your father?" I asked at last, feeling hurt.

"My father died. Car accident. He wasn't driving, it was a friend. Oh well. Life is strange."

It sure was, I thought. I noticed that Petros had begun rubbing his hands together nervously. Maybe we had made a mistake by wanting to meet his father. To search for him and find him.

"I imagine having Petros wasn't easy for you. Did you get married?" He smiled again, his eyes screwed up, his face creased with wrinkles, his neck red from the heat.

"No, it wasn't easy, not at all. But that's in the past. And here we are. Yes, I did get married. We're divorced now. Everything's fine for the two of us. My father lives with us. I see my mother a lot, and my aunt, and Osiris."

"Osiris?" He went pale. I realized that I'd made a mistake by mentioning Osiris in front of his wife.

"Perhaps you don't recall her, it doesn't matter." Yes, it mattered. I realized I had spent most of my life saying that nothing mattered, when the fact was that nothing had been more important in my life than my past. Never the present.

I thought we'd better say goodbye and "leave the door open," as we Cubans say, to meeting again sometime.

"Orestes, it's been wonderful to see you again and for Petros to meet you. Señora," I added, turning to his wife, "it has been a pleasure."

We hugged each other warmly. They promised to go see Petros at his concert by the harbor. We left, and that was that. As we went downstairs, I noticed the disappointment in Petros's face. I felt just as disappointed. Once we were in the street, Arsen shyly asked, "Want to get an ice cream? Or perhaps sit on the harbor seawall?" Trying to distract us.

Petros accepted the offer. "Ice cream's a good idea. It'll cool us off." He continued, "Mamá, now I've met my father. That was important for me, and I'm grateful you always spoke so well of him."

His eyes shone with tears. He put his arm around my shoulders, and we went to the harbor, following in our host's footsteps.

THE CONCERT IN Chania was another resounding success. Petros's father went to hear it with his wife. We saw them afterward in the changing room. Petros went over to shake his hand, and Orestes gave him an energetic bear hug.

"I want to let you know how sorry I am that I wasn't around when you were growing up, but I can see that your mother did a great job of it, for herself and for me. Thanks, Zé, thanks."

I gave a sigh of relief, knowing how happy these words would make Petros. We agreed that we'd stay in contact in the future and that we'd never, ever disappear again, neither of us—that was what Orestes added, though he'd been the one who had gone away forever and whom I'd never heard back from until then. I felt like reminding him, but I told myself, it's best to say nothing. Once again I kept my mouth shut.

We all ate out together at a restaurant on the harbor, facing the sea, as if we'd been in Havana. In some other era. An era when all this—dining happily with a pleasant view—was still possible.

Orestes and Marcia, his wife, gave us an affectionate and contented farewell. Petros, exhausted, went up to his hotel room; I told him I'd be up soon. Arsen asked me if I felt like a stroll. I said I'd be delighted.

The sky was a dark Prussian blue and the stars twinkled in ordered rows, like buttons on an ancient military uniform. The breeze caressed us in slow, measured beats. I could tell that from across the city you would be able to see all of Chania silhouetted against the magnificent, huge, yellow full moon.

We walked to the thick wall that stretches from the piers out across the water to the lighthouse. It was very dark. Arsen took me by the hand. I sensed that he had foreseen the thrill I would feel. I didn't reject his gesture but accepted it with delight.

"You might trip," he murmured as justification.

We sat on the wall, surrounded by the sea. The foaming waves, the starry blaze, and that immense moon illuminated the night.

I didn't know what to say, yet my lips parted automatically. "The time comes when women 'run to fat or turn to beanpole. Take to secret drinking. They marry men too young for them and get just what they deserve.'"

"I saw that movie, too." His exquisite hand ran along my head, my neck.

"What movie?" I smiled, foxy.

"*Ship of Fools*. That is Vivien Leigh speaking; it's a film by Stanley Kramer. There is also an extraordinary performance in it by Simone Signoret, looking more beautiful than ever. She plays a Cuban countess with a morphine addiction. A delight."

We looked long into each other's eyes. My eyes turned back timidly toward the stars. "All skies are the same," I told myself. "None is more beautiful than any other, the way they taught us to believe in Cuba. As if the sky over that island was the loveliest in the world. No, every sky is equally beautiful."

Arsen drew a small package from his messenger bag.

"It is a gift for you, to bring you back to your country."

It was a tiny boat carved from alabaster. A knickknack. I thanked him, deeply moved.

"But I do plan to return to Cuba. Did you doubt it?"

"No, not now."

"Did you ever?"

"At first. Now I know that you would never leave your father, not for anything in the world."

"No, I never would. Not him, not my mother, not my aunts. At the same time, Petros has a future here that he might not have back there anymore, on the island."

"Petros can apply for Greek citizenship, now that he has found his father living here. That would give him some protection. He could come and go whenever he wished."

"You don't understand, Arsen. When they close the doors on you back there, they close them for good."

"I know, but you will all do everything you can to make sure that doesn't happen. Please. I would like to see you again."

"I'd like that too, Arsen. I certainly would."

His hand now ran down along my arm, as he took my elbow again and helped me from the wall, that Malecón in the middle of the ocean.

I didn't want to go, had no desire to leave that place, please, don't let that moment ever end. I remembered being young, sitting on the Malecón seawall in Havana, imagining what I'd be like today. When I'd be as old as I am now. And here I am. This is me. Another woman alone. One more. An aging girl who had a few ideas and now doesn't even hope to see them carried out. Nor does she hope for anything from any man. Doesn't hope for love, doesn't want love anymore. Because, as in that movie, it may be that love has passed her by.

PARIS, JULY 14, 2014

About the Author

Zoé Valdés was born in Cuba in 1959. She took part in the Cuban pictorial movement of the 1980s through her work as a writer and art critic as well as an artist. Her texts were considered anti-establishment performances. Between 1983 and 1988, she worked with UNESCO and the Cuban Cultural Office in Paris before going into exile in France in 1995. Since her exile, she has been a screenwriter and assistant director of the magazine *Ciné Cubano*. Her bestselling novel *Yocandra in the Paradise of Nada* brought her international acclaim—she was once dubbed "the Madonna of Cuban literature"—and she has written many more works of fiction, nonfiction, and poetry as well as children's books. Her novels include *I Gave You All I Had* and *The Weeping Woman*, both published by Arcade. Winner of the Planeta Prize, Azorín Prize, Premio de Novela Ciudad de Torrevieja, and Premio Jaén de Novela, España, she has been named Chevalier des Arts et des Lettres in France and Docteur Honoris Causa Université Valenciennes France. She received the Tres Llaves (Three Keys) to the city of Miami in 2001 and more recently the Médaille Vermeil de la Ville de Paris. She lives in Paris.